THE BOOK OF WAS
(The Jack Waste Papers 2007-1994)

GREG BACHAR

Books By Greg Bachar

Three-Sided Coin
(Published Works 1990-2003)
2003

Sensual Eye
(The Jack Waste Papers Volume 1: 2004-1991)
2004

Curiosisosity
2013

Dumb Bell & Sticky Foot
(And Other Indulgences)
2013

Beans
(& Other Sundry Items From The General Store)
2013

The Amusement Park Of The Mind
(Essays On Thought, Feeling, Experience)
2013

The Writing Machine
(Writings On Writing: Occasional Ruminations
On An Intangible Legerdemain)
2013

The Sun Poems
2016

THE BOOK OF WAS
(The Jack Waste Papers 2007-1994)

GREG BACHAR

ROWHOUSE PRESS 2017

Inquiries:

Greg Bachar
P.O. Box 23134
Seattle, WA
98102-0434
U.S.A.

Cover: *Three Birds* by Matt Dyer

Photos: Greg Bachar

ISBN # 0-9719867-6-2

Acknowledgments

"Flowers Under Clouds," "Hiccup Of Desire," and "All Desire Is About Forever" were published in *Harness*.

I am here, watching, listening
with half of my soul at sea and half of my soul on
land, and with both halves of my soul I watch the world.
Pablo Neruda, *Agua Sexual*

What made understanding more difficult was the
permanent appeal of ambiguity.
Gellu Naum, *My Tired Father*

And there's heat in the sun / to see us through the rain
Do You Feel Loved, U2

THE BOOK OF WAS

WAS...1

A FIST IN A HAND

The Jux...5
A Fist In A Hand...6
Out Of Hock
(A.K.A. Basilica) (A.K.A. Something Peach)...7
Crush...10
Monday For Everyone...11
Strange Night, Strange Day
(A.K.A. University of Suffering)...12
The World...13
The Night That Never Was...15
Wild Blue Yonder...21
Foil (Jack Waste Album Track List)...23

THE ART OF POOL

A Story About Pool...26
Happy Pool Year...27
The Table...28
Bar Pool...29
Critics...29
The Final Failure...29
The Art Of Pool...31
The Brain Of Pool...32
The New Gravity
(A Jack Waste Public Service Announcement)...32

ALONE IN A ROOM OF THOUSANDS

Jack Waste's Cement X On Broadway...36
Imaginary Table Of Contents...37
Noc Noc Happy Hour, Hot Summer Day...37
Weirdville...39
Listen To What I'm Saying, Not What You're Hearing...39

Interview...41
Last Call!...41
A Modern Question For Artists Who Don't Want To Be
Celebritized But Want Their Work To Be Known...42
A Very Short Story (Until The Hands Warm Up)...42
The Funhouse Mirror Of Being...44
Chicken Katsu
(A Jack Waste Public Service Announcement)...45
Strata...46
Citizen of Inebriation...46
Roll Over Rover, Or:
Yawn, It's Just Another Martian Landing...47

KALEIDOSCOPE OF DESIRE

Kaleidoscope of Desire...50
Wet Feet...50
All Desire Is About Forever...53
Dissonance...55
Flowers Under Clouds...57
Strange Blanket...59
Super Bowl Sunday Eve...60
Something Out Of Nothing...63
Hiccup Of Desire...66
How To Be Mindful...68

THE BED OF MEMORY

Shed Your Containers!...71
The Cibstryction Of Drinks...71
Pleasures...73
Hefeweizen...73
Last Call...74

THE WINE STORIES

Trees...77
Crime...79
The Night...80

Let Go...81
Red Red Wine...83
The Future Of Our Past
(Say Something That Will Please Me)...85
Royal Palms...87
Foam Party...90
Gilligan & The Professor...93

LUCKY BEE

Lucky Bee (The Aesthetes)...96
To Be Known Or Unknown...97
Chapter One...99
Just A Dream...101
DHDHDHDH...102
People Made Of Clay...104
A Bit Of Calm In The Swirl Of Awkward Technicians...105
Saturday...106
The Old Are Dying,
The Dead Keep Giving The End Away...106
Within This Moment Is All Moments...107
Overarc (The Long March)...112
A Walk Down Broadway...117
Backwards Dream (Our Lady Of The Assassins)...119
Please Do Not Put Peanuts On These Steps (9/11/01)...121
October Night...122

THE RELUCTANT MONK

Advice To An Imaginary Daughter...126
The Reluctant Monk...127
A Day On Earth...128
What Use?...129
Evidence Of Decay...129
Into The Fray...130
A Token Of Our Appreciation...130

THE TROUBLES (W.T.O. RIOT DIARY)...133

SEATTLE STORIES (THE '90s)

World & Needle...173
Wild Bill...173
Number 10 To Nowhere...177
Snow...183
The Rolling Stones...185
Focus Group...187
The Richest People In The World...192
The President Of The Czech Republic...197
Terry Bradshaw...198
Dick Clark...199
Hilary Clinton's Salsa...200
Bill Clinton's Hand...201
"Sonics In 7!"...205
The Highlands...207
Tenniguiness...212
Codes...216
Longing (Desire)...220

WAS

In this City, things have recently begun leaving the places where they belong (or is it happening only in this writing?), much as times have begun to permeate one another (or am I merely becoming more susceptible to a phenomenon that has always been here?).
—Daniela Hodrova, *Prague, I see a city...*

The city of Seattle and Capitol Hill neighborhood described in this book (2007-1994) no longer exist. When Jack Waste arrived in 1994, Seattle was a dream. Capitol Hill was a dream. Now they are ghosts of dreams and you who read this are dreamers of ghosts.

When did the old Seattle die? There were many previous incarnations of the city, of course, but one could make a case for etching the year 2014 into the gravestone. In 2014, the Seahawks won their first Super Bowl and reached the previously unattainable peak.

Seattle was no longer an underdog city.

Tears of grief for its lost status didn't flow until the shock ending of the following year's Super Bowl. Blinded by championship hubris, the coaches elected to pass from the one-yard line with a minute left instead of giving the ball to Marshawn Lynch to run in for the win.

The pass was intercepted, the Seahawks lost, and Seattle fell hard from the top of the mountain. The next morning, the city woke up a bitter loser, no longer comforted by the reassuring blanket of its previous underdog status.

Old Capitol Hill died in 2014 too. Half Price Books closed in June. On 15th Video followed in September. Jack Waste had wandered the bookstore's aisles every Saturday afternoon since it opened in 2003. He had stopped by the video store several times a week since 1994.

Was: Ernie Steele's/Ileen's Sports Bar, The Easy, Ballet Restaurant, Café Septieme, Charlie's, Broadway Market, Fred Meyer, Jade Pagoda, Orpheum Records, Bailey/Coy Books, Pistil Books, Angel Thai, Broadway Grill, The Cinedome UA Cinema 150, Harvard Exit and Vodvil Theatres.

Was: Siam On Broadway, Red Apple Supermarket, 22 Doors, Rainbow Grocery, Kincora Pub, Piroshki On Broadway, The Gravity Bar, Hollywood Video, Steve's Broadway News, Baskin-Robbins, Capitol Club, Hi Score Arcade, The Vogue, Bad Juju Lounge, Piecora's NY Pizza, Satellite Lounge, Bauhaus Books & Coffee, Value Village.

Even the fast food is Was: Jack In The Box, Taco Bell, Burger King, Taco Time, Kidd Valley, Kentucky Fried Chicken, Godfather's Pizza, the Westlake Center food court.

Was: 211 Billiard Club, Speakeasy Café, The Gay Nineties, The Cloud Room, 700 Club, The Weathered Wall, Sit & Spin, I-Spy, The Kingdome, RKCANDY, OK Hotel, The Dog House Restaurant, Sorry Charlie's, the Kalakala.

Was: The Seattle Supersonics. Beast Mode.

Was, remodeled: The Canterbury, The Rendezvous, The Comet Tavern, Bill's Off Broadway, The Deluxe, Vito's.

Was, relocated: The Cha Cha & Bimbo's Bitchin' Burrito Kitchen, Twice Sold Tales.

Was, renamed: Moe's Mo'Roc'N Café, now Neumo's.

Linda's Tavern remains, but the pool table is gone and the bar is surrounded by condominiums. The Mystery Soda Machine, Dick's, Coastal Kitchen, Jamjuree, The Hideout, La Cocina, and El Farol all still remain, but for how long?

It's a different city, a different neighborhood. The next wave has arrived: new bars, new restaurants, new buildings, new people. Jack Waste wasn't one to rant against change, but the place he had attempted to call home for twenty-five years no longer existed, but then neither did that version of Jack Waste. The only constant in Seattle is the rain.

Was: the swoon of the analog full moon. No more jukebox setting the mood, no more standing in line to act the fool. No more back patio sky of "why ask why?"

No more sitting in the booth with you and you and you. No more I'll meet you there soon, I'm on my way, where are you?

Was: you and me and you and me and you and me. Loss is the key to the book of Was that everything will be.

A FIST IN A HAND

THE JUX

There's no future yet, just the moment, and the moment isn't really a moment, it's just a pause, a held breath, and a prayer rolled into one, a begging for the future to arrive, for something to *happen*.

Take your pad of paper and sit next to the pool table. Put some money in the jukebox, play some tunes. Avoid the familiar. Cross the street to the other side. Seek out strangers. Try the soup of the day. A few quarters will get you onto the pool table.

Nobody else in the bar is writing. You're really causing trouble now. Put the pen down. Listen to Joe Strummer. Eat some Cracker Jacks.

Think about the continuum of existence. Think about babies. There are babies everywhere. The babies are in charge. With your eyes closed and your headphones on, picture a line of infinite babies as a cosmic dance of endless geometric lines projected out into black space as rays radiating outward from within us.

Radiation.

All these babies are part of the continuum of the human race, each baby a link in a chain of succession spreading itself towards the far galaxies of the distant past and infinite future.

Open your eyes and look at your body stretched out on the bed. You are just one part of the continuum, but you contain half of the essence of life. We are bits in a bigger bit-thing, flesh machines on the march.

The babies are taking us to the stars, to the farthest reaches of time. Why don't you sign on the dotted line?

People stream through the door smiling Pabst Blue Ribbon smiles.

What do you know? Who knows?

Abstinence? Absinthe!

The paparazzi are everywhere.

Whatever! Stop staring! Check, check, cash.

A FIST IN A HAND

Jack Waste sat at the booth closest to the pool table at the top of the stairs from which one could see everything that happened and everyone that came and went, and wrote:

"To be a star means that you have to burn like a hard, gem-like flame. Do you burn like a hard, gem-like flame or are you a karaoke king or queen riding the penguin tails of someone else's vapors? The head of a comet is the most exciting place to be. Anywhere else you're just a follower.

Do you think you are really part of the band just because you know all the words to the songs? Were things always this way? Why do we spend so much on star love? Entertainment should be free, it's reality that we should pay for."

Jack put his pen down. He was done, for now. It was the hottest day of the year. Jack sipped his beer and watched the comings and goings. The noise around the silence was like a thief working in full view of everyone. Cue balls flew off the table and landed at his feet.

It was a regular night in the bar of the world, people coming and going and doing their thing, and yet he sensed they were all living through a time of change and transition from something written to something that was being written so fast they were unable to clearly see it.

Jack wondered if radical change would appear unfamiliar at first or if it would be immediately recognized the way one recognizes a stranger walking through the door as someone we'd like to meet. To this person Jack Waste wrote:

"Our interactions should be film-like, cinematic, awkward and brilliant, yes, the way spontaneous unscripted interactions are, but seamlessly beautiful. We should be jarred. We should be altered. We should be made to give pause. We should stutter step to each other's stallion steps.

We might have liked to be rare book dealers or professional tennis players. Do you feel like you've had many tastes of many things, but never the full menu? Do you sometimes feel like you are on the outside of things looking in, lagging behind, or trying to catch up? Other times, do you feel like you are at the center, the all-seeing eye?

Does your brain chemistry bless or curse you? Do you have memories of the womb? Is that why you swim in wine, music, poetry, and beer? Do you think of infinity? Are you humbled by the vastness of it all?

Perhaps we should pull a heist, eat in dark restaurants seated in private booths.

Let's be discreet. Life is a long goodbye."

OUT OF HOCK (a.k.a. BASILICA) (a.k.a. SOMETHING PEACH)

1.) It's hard to impress people who have seen it all or think they have seen all they are going to see, and neither of these people are impressed by someone who experiences a feeling for the first time when they have already felt it themselves.

2.) In normal parlance, the sensation most associated with experiencing something with fully open eyes for the first time is referred to as *wonder.*

3.) So it was when Jack's bartender at Linda's finished her shift with a self-mixed drink in hand that was unavailable at the bar and only possible because she had brought her own basil from home.

The Basilica: muddled basil, grapefruit juice, and vodka. Jack took one sip after she offered a taste and was transported in the direction of a destination he had never arrived at before.

And that was the night in a nutshell. Everything else that followed was aggrandizement and misapprehension.

4.) The guy two stools down from Jack had offended nearly everyone in the bar. He had proclaimed an offensive form of love for each of the servers and bartenders, none of whom were amused.

Jack told him his jokes weren't funny, that no one was listening, that one of the women was engaged, one was married, the other two had boyfriends, and most importantly, they were all "on the job," working hard so that everyone else might pretend that time didn't exist.

The guy opened the clarinet case he had just retrieved from the pawn shop across the street, bragged about what a good player he was, and told Jack that his father had been a well-known jazz musician down on 1st Ave. from the 50's to the 70's when Seattle was still "a real town."

Jack told him he wouldn't think he was much of a clarinet player if he didn't put his clarinet together and play something then and there.

The guy looked at Jack and seemed to understand something serious hung in the balance: he could walk out of the bar drunk and belligerent or he could play a song on his clarinet and walk out of the bar drunk, belligerent, and triumphant.

5.) Jack had watched a French romantic comedy the day before, *Love Me If You Dare*, in which Edith Piaf's "La Vie En Rose" was the film's recurring theme song, played each time in a different variation that reflected the state of the film couple's romance.

When the guy had his clarinet assembled, Jack asked if he knew the song.

"What key?!" he shouted.

"E," Jack said, pretending he knew what he was talking about.

"How does it go?"

Jack leaned forward and hummed the first few bars. The guy closed his eyes, took in a breath, and proceeded to play a perfect and beautiful rendition of the song.

After a few bars, he opened his eyes and looked at Jack as he played. Jack laughed. It was epic. He was pulling it off.

People sitting around them turned, leaned in and listened with smiling eyes. One of the bartenders muttered that it was obnoxious and needed to stop. The doorman walked over, tapped the musician on the shoulder, and said, "Dude, if you want to play that, you've got to play it outside."

The clarinetist smiled as he took his clarinet apart and said with an air of satisfaction, "I'm getting kicked out."

For just a moment, he sat triumphant and victorious, and then once again he began to insult the staff, telling one server that she was his wife and another server that she was also his wife and that another server would fall in love with him in the next ten minutes.

Finally, to the relief of everyone, he left. He packed up his case, cast a few repulsively sultry stares in the direction of the unresponsive bartenders and headed for the door.

Jack looked around the bar. It was a sloppy night. Everyone appeared to be very drunk. Everyone was talking loudly and no one was making any sense.

Based on the looks on their faces, it didn't look like any of the bar staff wanted to be there. They all seemed resigned to the fate the night had dealt them and did not see its beauty, but then, except for the Basilica and the clarinet player's rendition of "La Vie En Rose," Jack didn't see much beauty either.

6.) Jack asked the doorman why one wasn't allowed to play clarinet in the bar.

"It's against the rules," he said.

"What rules?" Jack asked.

"It's ANNOYING," the doorman said.

"Dude," Jack said, "in Mexico there are musicians everywhere and it's not against the rules."

The doorman looked around the bar with disgust in his eyes, then back at Jack.

"Dude," he said, "are we in Mexico?"

7.) Jack felt like he had overstayed his welcome with the night. He had only intended to have a beer, read the paper, and head home, but the clarinetist had caused him to stay beyond the pale limits of the evening.

Anyone with a shred of sense could tell there was no love in the air.

8.) In summation:

Jack witnessed the clarinetist play "La Vie En Rose." He tasted the Basilica and realized that the world still possessed flavors he had yet to experience.

These things gave him hope.

He didn't care that the doorman's mind was trapped on Earth. He didn't care that he had spent the night in a place that did not allow spontaneous expressions of creativity.

The door through which everyone came and went was just one door among many. There were other doors and other bars and other nights.

9.) Jack felt like finishing the night with something peach. He mentioned this to his bartender, who mixed up a concoction of things from different bottles, all topped off with a dash of peach schnapps.

Jack sipped from his glass of dreams and stared at the stars as the credits rolled and the night's theme song played. He closed his eyes and sang along with an imaginary roomful of strangers who were happy to join in.

CRUSH

The miniaturization of our existence is demeaning, so Jack Waste found it refreshing to arrive home and find that someone had left a map of the universe in the lobby's free pile.

The immensity of the universe humbled him when he studied it in his apartment later in the afternoon. Soon after, Jack lay down and napped for an hour with the television on, its volume turned down low.

Intermittent images interrupted his attempt at slumber: Paris Hilton's fear of going to jail, Lindsay Lohan's laughing eyes, a hockey game.

He did not dream, except to formulate a plan: go up to 15th to watch the end of the Cavaliers-Pistons game at The Canterbury, get some Thai food to go from Jamjuree, a few sundries at the grocery store, and return home to write. Jack took every conceivable shortcut there was to be taken between his apartment and 15th: up to 14th, over to John, diagonal through the Safeway parking lot to the path through the bushes near the edge of the property, across the street and under the bank's drive-in window roof, across the parking lot to the Subway sidewalk, then onto mainline 15th.

At the bar, a group of people from Ohio was rooting loudly for the Cavs. Detroit seemed to be playing soft and Cleveland was sharp. A cool breeze blew against the back of Jack's neck through the open bar window. He noticed an Oly poster on the wall next to the skee ball table.

"Now On Tap," the poster said.

The rest of the night proceeded according to plan until Jack climbed into bed and dreamed of the universe expanding and contracting like an infinite star-filled lung.

MONDAY FOR EVERYONE

Jack Waste hovered around Broadway, wondering what to do next. He needed a haircut but didn't feel like subjecting himself to even fifteen minutes of confinement.

He'd been to a friend's wedding the previous weekend and witnessed the holy matrimony.

He'd tried to work on the novels, he'd tried to read the books, but his immediate concern, mood, and distraction seemed to be one of unmet desire.

Had he been speaking the wrong language? Had he been hanging out with the wrong crowd? Was he in the wrong town?

Jack detached himself from all obligation and rode his bike down past the market, past the Bell Harbor Conference Center and Edgewater Hotel, all the way to the path that lead towards the grain towers and the *Seattle P-I's* revolving globe, and finally towards the train yards and what lay beyond. The wind blew strong against Jack's efforts. He felt no enthusiasm for the path he'd ridden many times before, but the water sparkled like diamond pendants, the air was crisp and clear, the sky blue. It was the first real day of summer, but now that he was out in it he wished he was nearing the final hill and heading back home, where he would write:

"I had ridden against the wind, past the grain towers, all the way to the railroad yards where the bike path grows thin between two chain link fences. If you plan to continue that way, then you are serious about making it to greener gardens. If not, you turn around and head back towards the city. Without headwinds to battle, I finally got into the zone of rhythm and motion. The bike became one with the path, and I with it, and it felt like I was really moving along. My blood was pumping, I was starting to feel alive, though still not necessarily connected with the rest of humanity. We are water pressing against water in all its forms. Ice does not meet boiling water well. Ice does not meet ice well. It's usually very simple, though: streams merge with rivers, rivers flow into the sea, the sea desires the river, and occasionally works its way upstream. If you want to meet someone new, surrender, be water."

STRANGE NIGHT, STRANGE DAY
(A.K.A. UNIVERSITY OF SUFFERING)

Jack walked through a hard rain to The Comet. There was no continuity in the air, everything seemed disjointed, and everyone seemed out of sorts, staring into a distance that could not coexist with everything in close proximity in such disarray.

A guy sitting on the stool next to his got up to go to the rest room. The girl he was with leaned over and asked if there were any other good bars in the area. Jack gave her a few suggestions up and down the street and asked if she was from out of town.

"No, I live in Wallingford," she said, "I don't come to the hill much." When the guy she was with came back and sat down Jack realized from what he could hear of their conversation that she was on a date, that her date was very drunk, and that she wasn't having a good time.

Jack heard the guy say he was from Belgium. Jack told him he lived in Belgium for a year, but the guy said he didn't believe him. Jack named the part of town where he lived in Brussels and a few bars he had frequented. The guy said he knew the places mentioned, but when Jack asked him where he lived, he only said that he lived with his mother to the east and waved his hand dismissively as if such details weren't important.

Jack wasn't sure what kind of game he was playing, so he turned his attention back to his beer, wishing he'd picked up on the bad date vibe sooner and spirited her off to a different bar where they might have waited out the rain and found some continuity together. Jack heard her tell the guy she was leaving.

"Why?" the guy asked. They leaned into each other like two people who didn't want anyone around them to know they were having an argument, so Jack didn't hear what she had to say. A minute later, they left together. She was laughing now. Off they went up the street.

Another woman at the bar checked her cell phone every ten seconds and looked towards the door like she was waiting for someone, but when a guy sat next to her, she only looked at it and the door twice more before putting it in her purse and turning her attention to him.

Jack looked over a few minutes later to see her rubbing her hands through his hair. Jack finished his beer and walked home in the rain, the whole world getting lucky without him.

THE WORLD

The world swirled around Jack Waste like a mad fog of mustard gas. He was tense, pulsing with pent-up energy, but he did not want to relax, he did not want to slow down to the pace of everyday life. Without a ship to sail out into unexplored regions, though, he was stranded. Jack grabbed a pad of yellow paper and Pablo Neruda's *Memoirs* and headed out into the day.

Angels immediately appeared in his path: the landlord sweeping near the back gate, an acquaintance waving to him from across the street, a homeless guy yelling at him with a big smile on his face like a long lost friend, "What's up, bro!!!"

Jack walked quickly down Broadway. He walked as fast as he could but it didn't feel fast enough to avoid being sedated by the slow motion crawl to nowhere. This was wasted time, time misspent. He wished he could edit out all the in between time like a movie and find himself at the next point in the storyline.

How many years of wasted in between time did it add up to over the course of one's life? All that getting from one place to another, all that standing in line, all the weekly laundry, waiting on hold on the phone... Add to that all the time spent watching television, watching movies, watching, watching, watching! Did watching count as *something?* Did it count as experience?

Jack stopped at the store to pick up a pack of his favorite pen, the Pentel Rolling Writer, black ink. He tried not to think of this as wasted time since the pens would lead to the page and its escape from time. He returned to Broadway and made his way to Ileen's. He knew it was going out of business, but he didn't know it had already closed.

An old drunk stared with a look of disbelief and confusion at the "Out Of Business" sign someone had scrawled and taped to the window. He turned and wobbled down the street, mumbling incoherently.

Jack pressed his forehead against the glass and cupped his hands around his eyes so he could see inside the dead bar. It was a dismal scene, all dirty floors and dark shadows and grimy dust-filled light filtered through grimy windows. He didn't look for long, just long enough to get a taste of what the place had become.

Archaeologists might dig into the site one day and attempt to determine how its ancient inhabitants had lived, but there was no way they could gather its memories from the mud and grit. Jack turned and walked down Broadway in search of another welcoming cave. He walked into Café Septieme and was given his choice of tables. The lunch crowd was back at work and the happy hour crowd had yet to arrive. He chose a booth near the back from where he could look at the wide-angle view of the passers by as they made their way down Broadway. The great movie of the world pulsed on. Jack took a sip of beer, uncapped his pen, and began to write: "The world swirled around…"

THE NIGHT THAT NEVER WAS

Does poetry embellish the night or does the night embellish poetry? Jack Waste was unsure whether to describe the night fully or to let the night fully describe itself, so he decided to try to do both, all the time wishing it could be different, that he was asleep elsewhere beneath the cool sheets of some foreign land's hotel bed.

Lookalikes

Jack Waste walked to Linda's, where the new Saturday night doorman who had been the new Saturday night doorman for several months still asked Jack for his I.D. "I haven't earned the 'wave-in' yet," Jack thought. "Old enough to be my own father, it gets tiring being asked to prove I'm old enough to buy myself a beer."

On his way to the bar, he thought his friend Salo was walking towards him, but just as he was about to say hello, the familiar face turned into that of a stranger. Standing near the jukebox deciding what to do with his night, Jack thought he saw his friends Sal and Dave walk through the door. "All right, Sal and Dave," Jack thought. It's cool when friends arrive and you had no plan to meet them. It wasn't Sal and

Dave, though, but Sal and Dave lookalikes. Jack looked around the bar. Everyone seemed to be a doppelganger of someone else. Even the strangers he didn't know and had never seen before looked like other strangers he didn't know and had never seen before.

Jack decided to leave, though a few blocks away, too late to turn back, he thought maybe he should have stayed, if only for that woman sitting in the corner booth with a book in hand who was also surveying the room, perhaps seeing lookalikes everywhere too, both she and he too distracted by the phenomena to spot the lone originals.

Convenience Store Notebook

Lines kept popping into Jack Waste's head. On his way downtown, he stopped in the convenience store between The Bus Stop and The Cha Cha. There was always a feeling of paranoia in this store, perhaps because its employees were so used to dealing with each night's array of crackheads, shoplifters, and drunks, that as soon as you stepped inside it felt like you were assigned one of these three late night Pine St. archetypes. Jack always felt like a shoplifter when he bought something there.

In the midst of a very small selection of stationary items, they had a pile of small blue notebooks, in the middle of which was a single red notebook. Jack picked up a blue one, put it down and picked up the red, which made him think of the devil, which made him put it down and pick the blue one up again. He didn't feel like dealing with anything remotely demonic even if the whole night was a sham orchestrated by just such a bored entity.

Never Get Off The Hill

Jack decided to get off the hill and walk down to The Rendezvous, a mistake he sensed almost as soon as he made up his mind. There was no energy in the air anywhere. He should have stayed put somewhere on the hill.

Once or twice a year Jack decided to get off the hill on nights like this with an equally empty vibe. It was almost always a mistake because anytime he decided to get off the hill it meant there really wasn't anything going on anywhere and that Jack had falsely convinced himself that there might be something going on somewhere else.

"Never get off the boat." Capt. Willard, *Apocalypse Now*

Yawning Beauty

Crossing the I-5 Bridge and walking down the hill towards the Re-Bar, Jack saw a twenty-something woman with blonde hair wearing a white fur coat yawning as she waited in her car to turn left. They looked at each other and smiled. Sitting at home later, Jack realized that it was the only hint of intimacy the entire night had offered and he wondered who she was and what the rest of her life would be like.

Sunrise At The Camlin

Jack looked up at the green Camlin Hotel sign and remembered his first morning there at his first job in Seattle years before. He looked at the top floor and pictured himself standing there eleven years earlier at the beginning of his first shift as breakfast busser. The sun was coming up over Capitol Hill as he looked at the neighborhood and wondered what his new life in his new city was going to be like.

There was chaos in the kitchen that morning. Instead of busing tables, he was desperately needed on the toast machine to help beat the breakfast rush. Later, at the end of service, the assistant manager said that he had "rocked on toast." It wasn't long before he was recognized as a competent employee and moved to room service and banquets. As he walked, Jack looked up at the banquet room windows and smiled as he thought about the night he was the sole waiter for Blue Oyster Cult's private banquet when they were in town to play a show and how they had tipped him a crisp fifty-dollar bill at the end of the night.

The Warwick Hotel

Jack walked past the Warwick Hotel and looked up at the windows of the top suites, where he had set up and served many banquets during his time as banquet waiter aboard that old tug of a hotel. Glimpses of memories flashed on the screen of his mind as he walked by: sleepy mornings after late nights out trying to show some enthusiasm for serving tour bus groups; cracking jokes with the rest of the crew during set-up and in the back hallways during service; eating shift meals in the small employee galley, all eyes up on the fuzzy TV screen in the corner; that New Year's Eve banquet when the manager, right after they had served the midnight champagne to the guests, grabbed several bottles himself and yelled for all the waiters to run with him to the alley, where they had their own toast and watched the fireworks explode around the Space Needle.

Jack pictured himself laughing with the other waiters as they clinked glasses and exchanged hugs and high fives until the fireworks ended and the banquet manager ordered them to get back to work.

Punk Rock

Jack was always looking for punk rock where it wasn't supposed to be and always surprised to find it lacking where it was.

It wasn't at The Rendezvous on this night, where he stood in line for ten minutes before the bartender took his order and then asked if Jack had anything smaller than the twenty he gave him to pay for his beer.

"That's all I've got," Jack said. The bartender looked irritated.

"Well, here's your change then," he said, "seventeen ones."

"It's harder to get a drink in this place than on the Titanic," he quipped to the woman standing in line behind him. She didn't smile.

Jack drank half the pint of beer while watching all the people he didn't know, which was everyone else in the bar, set his glass down on a table, and walked out the door intent on getting back to the hill for last call.

Down On Your Knees

Jack walked up 2nd Ave. He felt his left shoelace come undone and got down on his knee to tie it as a woman walked by. He looked up at her and smiled. She looked down at him and did not. There was nothing everywhere.

Talk To Me

Jack walked past Shorty's and wished he felt like a Veggie Chicago dog, but it was getting late. If he wanted to make it back to the hill in time for last call, he needed to keep moving. He walked past The Crocodile, where it appeared, like everywhere else, not much was going on. Jack turned left, then right on 3rd.

A homeless guy walking towards him said, "Talk to me, man."

"Talk to you about what, life?" Jack asked.

"Yeah, man."

"Life is ugly and beautiful," Jack said.

"I hear that," the guy said, and continued down the street. That stretch of street has always been the same, Jack thought. Haunted.

Dregs Of Heartbreak

At the next corner, he felt pangs of the last dregs of heartbreak about his recent break-up. A few days earlier, he deleted her number from his cell phone. It felt like the right thing to do.

It hadn't been an unbearable heartbreak, which led Jack to wonder if it was really heartbreak at all. He felt her absence, but now that some time had passed he only seemed to feel the absence of her absence.

"What are the laws of deletion?" Jack wondered, as he pondered his first break-up of the cell phone age. Two women stood next to Jack at the corner waiting for the light to change. One of them was on her cell phone and said to someone on the other end, "What are you still doing up?"

Burning Pots

For a good fifteen minutes as Jack walked up the hill away from downtown, the air was filled with a smell like a forgotten burned pot on the stove after all the water had boiled out. Then it was gone.

Gold Mine In The Sky

Back on the edge of the hill, he walked past the used bookstore on Olive near the highway entrance and stopped to look at the cover of some sheet music in the window, "There's A Gold Mine In The Sky," by Irving Berlin.

Jack decided this would be the theme song of the night and made a mental note to look it up online the next morning.

Against All Odds

As he got to within a block of his apartment, a drunk guy walked slowly on the other side of the street singing the Phil Collins song "Against All Odds."

Jack liked it for a while when it came out in 1983 and he was infatuated with both the actress Rachel Ward, who was in the movie, and a girl who lived up the street.

Flash forward to 2005 and the end of the night that never was. Twenty-two years later, the song was still in the air, as was Jack Waste. He climbed the stairs to his apartment, unlocked the door, went inside, and went to bed with the song stuck in his head. In the morning, he looked up "There's A Gold Mine In The Sky." "Yep," he thought as he read the lyrics.

WILD BLUE YONDER

You are in a dream. You have learned to sit still like an old man staring out at the ocean, each wave a memory crashing against your shore. The sound of the sea is tempered by layers of tinseled glass between you and it, but you do not worry about the waves of memory.

The bartender smiles and with a nod of your head a new glass appears. Your lips apply tender kisses and drink long and slow of the juice of love. Falling bombs do not bother you, except for the one that might fall right on top of the bar. Will you have enough time to laugh, to raise a toast and empty and empty your glass? Mushroom clouds do not frighten you. You've had dreams of them before, an explosion just off the horizon followed by the blast wave and radioactivity.

In this day and age of imminent threat, what does frighten you is that they haven't distributed cyanide capsules, just in case. There used to be a time when espionage really mattered and the last ditch bite down on the pill was all that stood between torture and sanity.

There's nothing to worry about now, though. It's Saturday happy hour. Angels cascade through the layers of tinseled glass. It must be a dream because none of them stop and walk through the door. You are waiting for *your* angel to arrive. Where is she? Will she come by land or by sea?

You have learned to nurse a beer like the old sea captain. Like him, you have learned there is no hurry. Slow or fast, you'll get there, you'll arrive, and early or late, you'll still be on time. Now the bar is getting busier, the line for elixir longer. What was once stillness is now a war, no longer the dream of an endless day after the fault line of dusk. The

Rolling Stones sing: "I'll come to your emotional rescue." You order another pint. The day no longer a blank possible slate, couples emerge to dance their silly dance. The world is no longer lost in dream, but in search of flesh.

One old man, the sea captain no longer in charge of a ship, stands guard at the pool table's stern, staring forward into its stretching wake. Young people say things like "um" and "uh huh" to fill in the old captain's silence, thinking the room needs noise, thinking his silence "uncomfortable." The young one who thought he might have an easy game is in for a surprise. The old captain wins easily.

Just when they were about to start another game, the young man looked out the window and saw his angel pass by. "There she is!" he thought, the game with the old captain no longer important. He apologizes as he heads out the door. The old captain nods and smiles. He needs no words, only jukebox reverie and the dance of cascading angels.

Someone has finally wound up the night and set it in motion. The old captain gathers his coat and makes for the door. No one knows where the old captain goes. You don't need to know, yet, but in your apprentice navigator's role, you have begun to suspect what the old captain means when he says he is going "out to sea."

He is going where sea and froth turn into bread and broth and old cracked photos on the wall tell stories ten and fifty feet tall. You suspect that the old captain does not miss the noise of the day when he leaves it behind. You suspect he has learned to love the silence of night and his dreams of the sea.

You suspect that the old captain knows the oceans speak all languages and in the end congeal into a single sea, the sea of memory, the silent shroud that if not chewed melts into longing. All over the world, billions eat and sleep and die. Now only you and the old captain know what the young men don't surmise, that the sea falls to rise, the sea falls to rise.

FOIL (JACK WASTE ALBUM TRACK LIST)

1. For A Good Time, Call
2. The Jux
3. Foil
4. Mix In The Drub
5. Colla Mosca ("With The Fly")
6. Foxy It-Claws
7. Solar
8. Fernet Branca
9. Snacks & Good Times
10. Ecstasy Comet
11. Unexploded Ordinance
12. A.K.A. "Home"

THE ART OF POOL

"Pool excellence is not about excellent pool. It's about becoming something."

Fast Eddie Felson, *The Color Of Money*

A STORY ABOUT POOL

Jack Waste lay on his bed, both smitten and disgusted with his decrepitude. He wanted to shoot pool, but it was Sunday and he knew a good game would be hard to come by given the range of tables that were an option in the neighborhood and the downbeat rhythm of Sunday nights. He understood the hill the rest of the nights of the week, but Sundays were impenetrable.

On this particular night, there wasn't a remnant of the rest of the week's celebratory glory in the air to suggest that anything but nothing would come of it. Still, he felt like getting out. He needed a chapter of his own story to walk arm in arm with rather than homebound cravings and untendered possibilities.

He tallied damages incurred and good times owed and at the end of this tallying he realized it was his duty to head out into the night in search of a game of pool. On the green felt of the table, all gray areas vanished and there was just you and the spheres.

After an hour in a booth at Linda's reading interviews with Andre Breton, though, not one person showed up to play, not even any of the regulars.

Two minutes spent inside the Kincora revealed there was no game to be had there either, and at Clever Dunne's, the table was occupied by vampire shadows and bat wings. It was not a night of angels.

Having found no game, Jack kicked at the piles of autumn leaves on the sidewalk as he walked home. Above him were the *ideas* of stars, hidden by a thick herd of clouds passing through town on their way to somewhere else. The weather people had been wrong. No storms had arrived, only clouds and wind.

He crossed Broadway and headed up the hill. Everything was aglow, but nothing was in play. Somewhere, great games were being played, but not here, not tonight, and if they were, he hadn't looked long enough to find them.

Tomorrow, the cycle would begin again. All over town, cue balls and stripes and solids slept and dreamed as Jack climbed into bed to wait for the slip and drift of sleep and the end of the gameless day.

HAPPY POOL YEAR

He had reached a really good place at the end of the year with his pool game. Jack didn't care about winning or losing from one game to the next. He realized it was all one big game that didn't have everything to do with him. If the other player made their shots, that's why they won, and if Jack missed his, that's why he lost.

He noticed that some players, though, talked smack while playing. They sharked and they sharked and they sharked, and sometimes they sucked you into their little mind game and you ended up losing your cool because of it.

At the end of the year, Jack didn't care what anyone said around the table. He was zeroed in on the shot and the next shot after that. He was focused on his grip, the head of the cue, and the angles, and he tuned everything else out.

When the new year started, though, he felt out of sync with the pool table and himself, so it felt good to find a little of his lost game at Linda's the previous night.

He lost on a pathetic scratch shot in the first game in which he rose up before following through and hit a miscued cue ball directly into the pocket while aiming at the eight ball.

Jack played the same guy again later. He was one of those types who felt the need to shark you by telling you to "have some balls" as part of their commentary about your game while you are playing.

Jack beat him outright and then when he played him again later and was getting into the flow he beat him going away with three consecutive difficult angle shots. The guy seemed so perturbed by his change in fortune that he didn't shake Jack's extended hand afterward and walked off with a disgusted look on his face.

Jack felt done for the night at that point but had to play again since he had won and it was his table. His next opponent was a guy who didn't seem to have much of a sense of humor and appeared to really want to beat him. He was taking his shots way too seriously and spent so much time lining them up that Jack thought perhaps he was trying to shark him by deliberately slowing the game down.

Jack hit several good shots in a row and felt momentarily unbeatable and back on his game. In the end, he missed all his remaining shots by a hair, which didn't bother him because he knew he was finding the lost angles again, but it ended up costing him the game.

"That guy was TOO serious," Jack thought after he left the bar to walk home. Part of the mental game, though, is how you play when you know your opponent thinks you're pretty good. If they visibly want to beat you, it means you have the upper hand, and even if they do end up beating you, you walk away knowing that when you play them again they'll still be thinking the same thing, and you can use that to your advantage.

"That being said," Jack thought, we ARE talking about hackers and choppers at Linda's here, not the national tournament circuit."

THE TABLE

You need to step away from the table to be able to see the table. You need to step away long enough or far away enough to be able to see the table as if for the first time. Just step away. You aren't connected to it. You aren't connected to anything. You're free. Move to a new town. There are friends everywhere.

BAR POOL

Jack Waste wrote, "My hunger for the blood of victory and defeat has waned. Winning and losing no longer matter. The thrill of the game is gone, at least for tonight. I have schooled and been schooled. I have sunk magnificent shots that none of my friends were there to see. I have squandered certain victory on waylaid shots when my friends were standing by to witness my shortcomings. I have walked into bars where I knew no one and put my name up on the board to play. The only thing left is to own my own table. The only thing left is mansion life.

When I've played my best I am not thinking, just acting and reacting automatically, breathing, lining up shots, taking shots, moving around the table aware of every angle, making a run, lost in the blur and cacophony of the choreographed symphony of the night, endless beauty, stopped time, hyperspace, liftoff, eight ball in the corner pocket."

CRITICS

"Jack, you suck," Rick stated unequivocally. "I don't think you're very good," Stefanie stated with apparent disappointment the first time they played. "You're not a good pool player," Casey stated casually but firmly, as if thinking out loud about an idea he wasn't fully invested in but knew to be fact. And yet, while they may have won some games they played, he had also won some too and said nothing afterwards about their shortcomings on the table. He thought it better to play than to play and have a say.

THE FINAL FAILURE

The Final Failure is when something happens to you for the absolute last time that you can look it in the eye and smile as if everything is all right. It's not. Regardless of how healthy, rich, or loved you might feel, your life is dribbling away in drops of blood, oxygen, and untendered love. You know what I mean.

We don't REALLY need to talk about this, and after all, this is a chapter about pool, not desire, so why should we allow ourselves to be distracted from the subject at hand? Because of this: you either realize the moment or you realize the moment after the fact because you were playing it cool when you should have played it hot.

There is a point in the night when you realize you've had enough. You're tired, the noise is noise and not music, and you do not feel wise and above it all. You shoot a few games of pool, make a few brilliant shots, and win a couple games with attitude and conviction. In short: YOU RULE.

Then you lose and put your name up on the board and go back to where you were sitting to watch the parade of humanity pass in front of you. People stream through the door and you watch to see if anyone enters that you don't know yet but who you imagined might one day recognize YOU.

A friend is talking. The jukebox is loud. You are keeping half an eye on the pool table and those playing and half an eye on the room at large. You are starting to think that perhaps you should just go home, that there's nothing here, just a shell of a room and some noise.

Who wrote the master plan? And if there is no master plan, why do things happen as they do, so beautifully and exactly as they are supposed to? No one knows. Moments come and go, you're either in the moment or you're not. The moments that seem the most true are the ones you find yourself acting on as if by automatic design.

Then there are the moments you realize after the fact, three seconds to three days to three years later. What does this all have to do with pool? Read on.

Don't play pool if you really don't want to or if the people playing pool at the table that night aren't people you really want to play with. Go sit with your friends instead or meet someone new or sit in the corner and make plans for the future or work on your novel.

If there's no sense of "danger" and excitement around the table, don't bother. Most Friday and Saturday nights are "Amateur Nights," but if you do go out, pretend you're not the Pool Hero you want to be and let the amateurs have their way with their sloppy play.

Victory is a tasteless dish when served unthawed. Wait until the table is hot and then put your name up on the board.

Stare longingly at the table and allow yourself to visualize the future glories to come.

The horizon is nearer than you think. Time is a trick of the senses. Stay hungry. Stay ready for the fray. Suddenly tomorrow is today.

THE ART OF POOL

Don't ash on the table. Don't put your drink on the table. Don't toss your stick in disgust. Don't ask if anyone has quarters—bring your own. Don't be fascinated with your victories—get ready for the next game. Sometimes you have to go for the kill. Sometimes you have to ignore fame and glory and take the makeable shot. Sometimes you have to go for fame and glory and take the spectacular shot. Winning on an opponent's eight ball scratch is still a victory. Don't give in to illogic. Play like you're tired (relax). Never shoot when Joy Division's "Love Will Tear Us Apart" comes on the jukebox when you're about to shoot. Say "excuse me." Don't talk to friends while playing against a stranger. Ignore distractions. There are no rules—just play. Some nights you can't find your game—did it ever exist? Master the break. Are you playing against your opponent or yourself? Why did you lose? Why did you win? Don't feel defeated if you lose, just feel like you lost. Play the angles. Play the ball, not the opponent. You don't "deserve" to win—it's not luck and it's not accidental.

THE BRAIN OF POOL

Figure the angles. Get a grip. Line up the tip. Don't act pissed or surprised when you miss a shot. You missed it for a reason. What's the reason? If it was easy, it wouldn't be hard.

Ignore the sharks. Example: a guy misses the eight ball, leaving you with one and the eight ball to make for the win, says "good game," puts his stick down and adds, "I lined it all up for you."

You look at it. It *is* all lined up, the one ball next to the corner pocket, the eight ball next to the side. And then you miss.

"C'mon, man, what's wrong with you?" the shark says, and wins the game, having successfully *made you think*.

Ignore the sharks.

Don't think you're going to win until you've won. You're not really playing against your opponent. It's just you, the angles, and the table. Check your mental.

THE NEW GRAVITY (A JACK WASTE PUBLIC SERVICE ANNOUNCEMENT)

Dear Reader,

Gravity shifted this week. Don't trust anyone who says they didn't feel it. If they didn't feel it they weren't paying attention. I felt it all week on the pool table, but it wasn't until my pool shark friend started sending balls awry and two other players admitted that their games had also gone south that I realized something was really up.

I mentioned the shift to my friends around the table but they all gave me "whatever dude" looks. Well, trust me, friends, gravity shifted this week, and it shifted in our favor.

Last night, a guy appeared outside the bar wearing a suit and a devil mask. He looked through the window, pointed at people, and gestured invitations for various women to join him.

When no one complied, he removed a short but thick chain with a padlock on the end from his inside suit pocket and rattled it against the glass.

When I left the bar to go home, a guy standing on the sidewalk where the devil had stood earlier exclaimed to his friends, "I'm an angel, motherfuckers!"

His friends laughed at his declaration. What did this angel/devil tug of war outside my favorite bar mean? When I got home, I went straight to bed.

The next day I went bookstore shopping in the early afternoon, took a nap until early evening, then headed out to deal with the issue of gravity around the pool table.

A guy who plays a lot of Saturday nights was there. He played a brilliant game, beating the bar shark by coming back from behind with enough momentum to win the next five games going away.

I lost a rusty awkward game to him in which I could not grasp the basic concept of my own geometry. I played again, this time a little better, but my shots alternated between brilliant and pathetic.

Another pool table friend stopped by between shots to inform me that his game was also off. I wasn't sure if he was sharking me or if he really meant it because after he told me that he went on a little run.

When it was my turn, I made some sloppy shots followed by some deliberate defensive shots when I had no clear angles to keep him away from easy shots. He started missing then and I chipped away until my spectacular-LOOKING but actually easy eight ball bank shot into the corner pocket won the game. I thought that maybe I had learned something about the new gravity but now it was my turn to break.

I don't like to break. I need to go away to some distant island of pool tables for a long, long time to just practice my break. The bar pool shark had this to say when I asked for his advice about breaking: "Break hard." Well, I "break hard" every time but sometimes the stick glances off the ball, sometimes my arm breaks towards the wall, and other times I hit an only slightly solid shot that doesn't put anything into any of the pockets.

I had a good break for a change and played another sloppy game early on, only to come back solid and smooth, everything going into cinematic slow motion as I grew even more comfortable with the new gravity, then won a second game in a row the same way as the first followed by a third game the same as the first and second.

I had only won three games in a row once before. That other time was in the early afternoon immediately after waking up from a nap and deciding that I didn't want to cook dinner at home.

I was so hungry as I played while waiting for my food to arrive that I did not care about pool and every shot was a brilliant impossibility made possible by the looseness of my body and mind. I beat three good players in a row and one of them suggested that I was a "shark." I'll let him think that even though he's beaten me more times than I've beaten him. All the pool movies I've watched emphasize talking shit to your opponent and betting large amounts of money. I suggest shaking your opponent's hand before playing and making them shake your hand before breaking if they don't offer it themselves.

Beyond that, all should be silence and interior monologue. I want to see world leaders shoot pool. I don't want to hear about another summit, treaty, speech, or debate. Let it all be decided on a pool table.

I think I've watched all the pool movies that have been made. *The Color Of Money* is the best, and the one that has the most to teach you about pool *and* life.

The new gravity, though, is something you're going to have to figure out yourself.

Stay tuned,
Jack Waste

ALONE IN A ROOM OF THOUSANDS

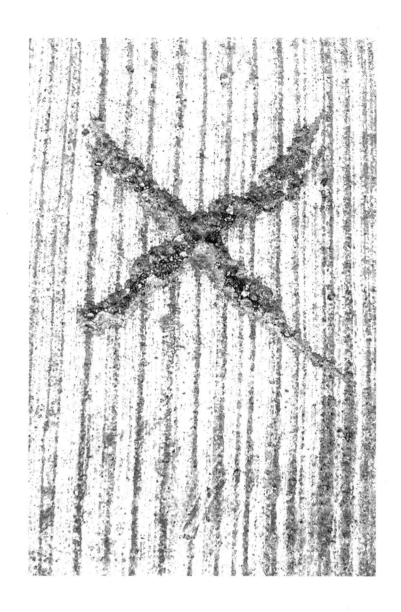

Jack Waste's cement X on Broadway.

IMAGINARY TABLE OF CONTENTS

1. Age Of The Odd Man Out
2. She Has To Be Brave And She Has To Call Because That Extra Ticket In Her Pocket Is The Ticket To My Heart
3. Fake Heavy
4. Tired Of Playing It Cool.
5. Why Do We Need Hand Stamps?
6. Winter: Absurdity
7. Spring: Revolution
8. If You Catch Me, Will I Fall?
9. Jukebox Music
10. The King Of Fun
11. Mystery
12. What The Doorman's Reading
13. Hate Is Just Love Turned Inside Out
14. A Substitute For The Absence Of Fun
15. The Fifth Duplicate

NOC NOC HAPPY HOUR, HOT SUMMER DAY

Rolling down through zero-g, everything real is an illusion and every illusion is real. A bored doorwoman indifferently checked ID's without looking up at anyone's faces. Undiscovered supermodel or lost in space? It was hard to tell. Everyone wants to be part of the Hollywood Machine. The DJ played Bob Marley to remind us what's real. Our time is a scale model interpretation of glories long past and glories yet to be imagined. Living a cinematic life doesn't feel the same as watching a cinematic life on the screen. Real life arrives uncooked. Celluloid is delicious.

We need to cut our rent and stash our cash. PBR Street Gang, PBR Street Gang, our insides are inside out. Life was live when Jimi was alive, not Han Solo'd in carbonite on

Broadway. The beer man has arrived and rolls kegs through the door. We're alive, we're alive, we're alive.

Where can this lead? How far can it go? We crave so much but sit around staring instead of making things new. We were once Earthshine, Moonshine, Sun Queen, Sun King, but now we don't touch what we aren't prepared to embrace. False dabblers everywhere, time saboteurs. Are you a dabbler too? Go to the zoo. This notebook is cooler than you.

We want dusty desert motels, a trailer in New Mexico, a black and white TV that only gets two stations, enough desert stretched out back to shag golf balls towards the mountains and into the purple night.

What's your RPM, how slow can you go, do you fake your glow, do you con your show, we want to know. Pretend you're a giraffe. Undo your muscle memory and join the fun.

The third one they give you never resembles the first. The little dog running around no longer seems cute. It doesn't feel like we're waiting here to leave for the moon. It's just an afternoon. Basic human logic is flawed. We should want to operate using Advanced System 19. You know what I mean. Music is the attack we've been holding back.

Jack Waste capped his pen and looked around the room. The doorwoman yawned.

"Hey, what's that you were writing in your notebook that whole time?" the guy sitting on the stool next to him asked.

"My novel, man," Jack said.

"Your NOVEL? What's it about?"

"You know…reality."

"You mean YOUR reality?"

"Yeah, dude," Jack might have said, but the guy then knocked his pint all over the bar and partially on Jack. End of conversation. Idea: a bar just for writers. If you're not writing, you have to leave.

WEIRDVILLE.

You go out for an early dinner but get caught up in the nightlife: people talking, the cue ball clicking, a game up on the screen. Everything seems possible if you can just write long enough to live your memoirs.

Chances are given to everyone but only taken by those who know how to recognize them. Statistically, how many people live in the moment and how many live outside? If there are possible parallel pasts, then there are possible parallel futures. You've just got to recognize the one in which you're not left behind.

Every jukebox song is a history of moments. You are only here for so long. There are only so many moments like this. It's a nice moment, but a familiar song. You want a soundtrack of music from the future.

The after hours party was nothing to aspire to but that's where the night led. The general consensus was that you all should have stayed home. Everyone looked good under black light, not so good in regular light. Walking home, the morning bird sang.

You thought it was singing for you, but when you stopped to listen, off it flew.

LISTEN TO WHAT I'M SAYING, NOT WHAT YOU'RE HEARING

You think you have earned the *right* to be entertained. You think it is okay after a long day of work to reward yourself with some time to "veg." And then tomorrow you will do the same, and on the weekend you will pay to watch a movie, and all over the world, people will spend millions of dollars to see the same film, and the week after that, and the week after that, and still we will blame government and our leaders for everything that is wrong in the world. You have been programmed into a routine of submission and expenditure of resources. You have considered but never followed through on the possibility that another way to live might exist, that it might be better to spend your money and time on creative *production* instead of consumption. By accepting things as they are, you were defeated without even knowing you were at war.

We are robots. We are machines. When one of us goes down we cry as we are programmed to do and then continue on. We are programmed to mate and reproduce and pleasure ourselves. Our chemicals create our reality. Who programmed us? We have spirit, but need to be creatures of action. Thought is our weapon that turns word into action. We need to create to evolve. If we know we are programmed, then we should also know that we can rewrite the program. We've got to *use* time so we don't lose the time we've got to use.

Everyone is not equal. The world is run by the healthy and strong. Humanity's hedonism of denial is only able to manage the acceptance of a narrow spectrum of ideals: beauty, strength, visual appeal, a positive attitude, but reality, REALITY, is luck of the draw.

There needs to be a revolution of thought against the concepts of credit card bills, making payments on time, late fees, and "making do." Why is there such an acceptance of the models handed down to us? What if we all just didn't pay? What happened to the ancient concepts of discovery and self-invention? Ice melts and becomes something else. It could be a river or that part of the sea you always wanted to see. What will happen when the tide comes in? That cycle of turning, the inevitable moment. Are you trapped in pop culture? Have you forgotten the fundamental elements? Neither better than humanity or a true outsider (you like a good sandwich and fries just like everyone else) it just seems like there should be something more. Don't throw away tomorrow today. A poet should embrace strangeness and wonder. A poet should see beyond what others see. A poet should see in 6-D.

INTERVIEW

Q: Are you interested in the past? Nostalgia? Awareness of present moments passing that will never be again? *Explain*.

Q: Are you interested in what is going on now? *Explain. Provide Specific Examples*.

Q: Are you interested in what has yet to happen? *Provide Specific Examples*.

Q: Are you interested in what doesn't exist yet, that which has yet to be invented? What are some of these things? *Provide Seven Distinct Examples*.

Q: Are you interested in the abstract and/or absurdity? *Use Abstraction Or Absurdity To Explain Yourself (Or Both)*.

Q: Are you interested more in yourself or in others? *Explain & Prove It*.

Q: Describe your vision of a "new reality." *In Two Long Paragraphs*.

LAST CALL!

Jack Waste was standing in line after last call had been made.

"Do you think about death every day?" he heard someone ask. Jack turned around to find that the question had been addressed to him.

"Jesus, dude," he said to the guy, "That's a helluva thing to ask at this time of night."

"No, I'm serious," the guy insisted, "Do you think about death every day?" He looked like he was no more than twenty-five, and though he had asked a pretty heavy question he had a look of amusement in his eyes. Jack wondered what force of the universe had arranged this interaction when the bar was swimming so pleasantly beneath the weight of the full moon.

"Sometimes," Jack said, "but not at last call."

"I think about death every day," the guy said.

"You're gonna live a long life," Jack said. The line moved forward a bit.

"I think it's weird," the guy continued.

"What's weird?" Jack asked.

"I mean, it doesn't make sense. We're here, and then we die. I don't get it. It's weird."

"Yeah it is," Jack agreed, "But we're here now. Look around you, man."

The guy didn't look. "Dan," he said.

"Huh?"

"Dan," he said again, holding out his hand. Jack shook his hand, told him to lighten up a bit, and returned to his friends and what was left of the night: the last game of pool, the last song on the jukebox, last jokes, last laughs, last glance across the room at the woman with smiling eyes.

"There are better things to think about," Jack thought, "especially at last call."

A MODERN QUESTION FOR ARTISTS WHO DON'T WISH TO BE CELEBRITIZED BUT WANT THEIR WORK TO BE KNOWN

Do you HAVE to be seen to be heard?

A VERY SHORT STORY (UNTIL THE HANDS WARM UP)

As he rode his bike through the cold rain, his hands numb just minutes after beginning the ride home, Jack Waste tried to find a reason behind the night's events. He came up with two: 1.) Sometimes you go out to realize you wanted to stay in; 2.) Solitude on film is poetic. Solitude in real life without a camera crew is not.

The day's light had never risen beyond a pale shade of gray. This did not bother him but when it began to get dark for good, Jack found himself restless for company he did not have and groceries that weren't in his fridge.

The weather had driven people into their homes. Only six or seven people shopped for sustenance at the store. He gathered all the ingredients for a perfect meal, but none of them felt right. The idea of being cooked for while sitting among other people appealed to him more. His apartment felt uninviting and he was fighting off a cold, leading his body and mind to deviate from its normal satisfactions, so he put away his groceries and headed out. Wild salmon, asparagus, and potatoes fried in olive oil would have to wait.

As soon as Jack ordered a beer and asked to look at the menu, though, he knew that he wanted to be back at home assembling the meal he had imagined in his head and shopped for at the store. His stomach needed immediate reassurance, though, so he ordered a greasy veggie burger and fries that left the pit of his stomach with a roiling feeling when he was finished.

He paid his bill and got on his bike to ride home. He saw a couple friends standing on the sidewalk and waved at them but did not stop. When he got home, he could still hear the noise of the bar in his head, the conversational din, and the jukebox, but they were soon replaced by the winter mantra of falling rain, sirens, and distant train horns. As his hands warmed up, the night slipped away.

He thought about the night he had left behind and the night he had found and wondered what it would look like on film. Man goes alone to a bar. People move around him, drink, talk, laugh, shoot pool, the jukebox plays, it's all a dream and everyone is in the know. Solitude on film is poetic. In reality, it is cold hands, an upset stomach, and the promise to stay home tomorrow night and do things right.

THE FUNHOUSE MIRROR OF BEING

Jack Waste wrote, "The flaw in your thinking is the word "if" and the question "can I?" You need to wonder what has made you so passive that you feel the need to ask these questions. What right do you have to surrender your own free will? No one granted you this, and yet year after year you throw your money away into entertainment and wasted time. What is the matter with you that you are so bored with the versions of reality presented to you? Get off the couch. Stop asking questions."

Years earlier, just after Jack had moved to Seattle and when he was beginning his first job that would get him enough money to start his new life, he was staying at his brother's apartment on top of Queen Anne above the train yards. One night, his brother's roommate, after several beers and a few whiskeys, announced drunkenly, "Dude, we're winners without winnings."

Jack smiled and nodded his head. It was a beautiful line, poetically, but he was quite sure it didn't apply to him. The mathematics of the phrase only added up, after a few actions of subtraction and addition, to equal "Dude, we're losers." Jack was quite sure this title did not apply to him. How could it? He was just starting out in the new city. Everything was full of possibility, and within weeks, he would find steady work, a girlfriend, and his own apartment.

Now, years later, he still had steady work and a nice apartment, but the girlfriend was long gone. Jack didn't feel like a winner, but neither did he feel like the champion of the world. He'd had his share of "winnings," though, in the years since the night of the "winners without winnings" line and thought that perhaps he was at least breaking even.

Up above the Earth, astronauts worked in zero g on the space station. Tomorrow was Friday the 13th, Saturday was Valentine's Day, Sunday was Sunday and Monday was a holiday. Winter kept pushing in.

It had been a night with no first sentences, only middles and beginnings realized after the fact when it was too late to get them down on the page. "The Funhouse Mirror Of Being" popped into Jack's head as a possible title for the night.

He felt like Jeff Daniels in *Something Wild*, Jeff Goldblum in *Up All Night*, and Griffin Dunne in *After Hours*. It was not an entirely good feeling. Everything was molasses. Time had slowed, stopped, or disappeared entirely.

He'd felt four hours behind the day all day and now it was already tomorrow. There was no way to catch up and no way to get ahead.

There was disconsolation everywhere, a thick mulch of sirens and punks falling off their skateboards against cold cement while the sliver moon smiled a yellow denture grin and winked its one good eye.

There was no reason to be anywhere but home, but even home felt like nowhere. It was a nowhere nothing night.

CHICKEN KATSU (A JACK WASTE PUBLIC SERVICE ANNOUNCEMENT)

Jack Waste wrote, "All previously attributed beliefs are outdated. We need new definitions. Specific sets of chemical reactions lead to specific states of mind. Feelings are real, but now that we are able to identify why we feel the way we do after Chemical Set A plus Chemical Set B come together in our mind's chemistry interaction sets, our viewpoint is irrevocably changed. We are liquid, chemicals, and compounds, combined in accidental chains, and we are moving forward.

As scientific advances speed up and we decipher the codes of the body and mind, we are only furthering the possibilities of our survival. The only realistic option is to say *yes* to it all. In another fifty, hundred, or thousand years, future humans won't recognize these primitive bodies we inhabit today. To be "post human" does not suggest we will lose our humanity. It suggests that we will become a new form of ourselves that we can't imagine yet. Why would we reject OURSELVES?"

45

STRATA

Sometimes you break your own rules and stay too long or choose the wrong place to stay too long in the first place.

Sometimes you gamble and talk to someone new who turns out to be the wrong person to talk to when the only reason you talked to them in the first place was the knowledge you achieved from talking to someone new in the past.

Sometimes you set out into the night with one thing in mind and return home with an entirely new set of rules the night taught you.

Sometimes you find out that everyone else is experiencing exactly the same thing as you are and sometimes you find out no one has any idea what you're talking about.

And if you ever find yourself backstage at a rock show, remember that only the band is supposed to be there. That's why it's called *backstage*.

Leave immediately, unless you find yourself kissing the most beautiful person there.

CITIZEN OF INEBRIATION

I want to do what I want to do through the bass to you. WAIT FOR FURTHER COMMUNICATION. God, what does my left hand get? God, what does my left hand do? If this is hell I think I'm in heaven. If I had a window I could see the sun. I AM EMILY DICKINSON IN REVERSE. Don't read this book if you're in a rush. Slow down, it's full of bottles and casks that give birth to the empty glass. I've learned a new speed: slow. Try to keep up. POETRY IS A SHAM. GO OUT AND RENT A CATAMARAN. FORGET MY INFRASTRUCTURE, YOU MAKE ME SUFFER HISTORY'S ANTECEDENT. GO IN THROUGH THE EXIT! ACT LIKE YOU BELONG!

Don't shout!

ROLL OVER ROVER, OR: YAWN, IT'S JUST ANOTHER MARTIAN LANDING

Jack Waste wrote, "How can you express an honest and open indifference to our rovers landing on Mars? We're there. Make yourself feel it just for a bit. Earth and its Earthlings aren't going anywhere, but your mind is free to travel. The poet attempts to see these things and put them into words. The poet attempts to send the imagination where he or she knows the body will never go. Why imprison your mind with jaded sensibilities? Open up to infinity. Infinity is where it's at."

KALEIDOSCOPE OF DESIRE

KALEIDOSCOPE OF DESIRE

Jack Waste wrote, "I wanted to go to war against war but I didn't know if war was wrong or right, I mean, I knew there was a threat, but it seemed more important to make new friends than to make new enemies. That was where I was in my own life, anyway, even if I was quite inept at meeting people. I wanted new friends and figured that if we could put ourselves in a position to party, dance, eat good food, and listen to music together that we could all come to some agreement over after hours breakfast. Was this naïve?

Nobody knows anything anymore. We are so trained to witness packaged versions of reality that we are no longer able to immerse ourselves in conventional sincere moments without the facilitation of some form of electronic media. We are so lost in nostalgia for what we've seen happen in movies and TV shows that we don't know what to do when faced with situations that don't fall into the shape of those templates. Thoughts paralyze our actions as we try to emulate the imagined realities of films past. The future with no name and no memory is where it's at. Let's go *there*."

WET FEET

Jack Waste wrote, "Wet feet are not the same as cold feet, but sometimes one leads to the other. Living in Seattle, you find yourself walking in the rain a lot. Before you know it, your socks and feet are wet through your shoes and the rest of the day or night is comprised of circumstances based solely on the fact that your feet are no longer entities separate from the deluge outside.

They are *wet*, but you go about your day or night pretending as if they are not, and after several years of living in Seattle, wet feet no longer cause any panic or complaint. Still, there *is* a psychological effect on your whole being that is based on whether your feet are wet or dry, and wet feet alter one's clarity of thought and action."

Jack Waste capped his pen and slumped against the back of his chair, fully aware of the weight of the moment while listening to Caetano Veloso sing "Cucurrucucu Paloma" on the soundtrack to Pedro Almodovar's *Talk To Her*.

The last thing on his mind this particular night was company, but when he heard his name called outside the window he was happy she was once again arriving. He opened the window and looked outside. She was standing on the sidewalk below smoking a cigarette and was wearing a white knit cap with a big snowball bob on top.

"Coming in?" he asked. She nodded yes.

She showed up outside his window every now and then and either called his name or threw a small rock to get his attention. She lived just three blocks away up the hill, so it was not unusual for her to stop by. For her to stop by after ten o'clock at night, though, usually meant that something had gotten to her and needed one-upping.

As he approached the front door in the lobby, she pressed her nose against the glass and made a funny face. He opened the door, held it for a moment until she was inside, and walked back down the hall towards his apartment. She followed behind, neither of them speaking. There was a pile of clothes on the floor in front of the door. He pushed it out of the way with his shoe. The clothes that did not cooperate and budge he shoved aside with the edge of the door. They bent and slumped without showing any sign of annoyance or cooperation, so he ignored them and invited her to step carefully over the pile.

She looked around the room, said, "Everything's been rearranged," and fell in a heap on his bed. He had moved his good television into the closet in an attempt to disconnect from the television world for a while. On top of his stack of three bass amps, he put his nine-inch pawn shop television that didn't have a remote control. If he wanted to watch TV, he would have to get up and turn it on manually. He had also moved the bed towards the center of the room and created a little social area with his loveseat and coffee table in the corner the bed formerly occupied. When he stood back to look at the new arrangement, he felt like the room was able to breathe a bit more "roomily" and hoped the change might somehow introduce some positive changes into his life. A few minutes later, she called his name.

Jack lay down on the bed next to her. After she told him that she had stood in front of the beer coolers at 7-11 pondering a drink after almost a year of sobriety before deciding to walk to his apartment instead, she said, "drinking only leads to suicide." She was in a faraway state.

"Feeling any better now?" he asked a few moments later.

"It helps," she said, referring to what he wasn't sure.

She said she was feeling crazy, that she had talked to an old boyfriend on the phone, and that he had been distracted and unable or unwilling to give her the attention she needed. When she raised her head from Jack's pillow and said she felt like she was going insane, her eyes were puffy but full of life. Eventually, she seemed to be in better spirits than when she had arrived and hugged him tight in the lobby before leaving. He asked if she wanted him to walk her home.

"No, I'm all right," she said, and walked slowly up the street and into the night.

Jack had all the makings of a dinner in his refrigerator, but none of them appealed to him. He wanted Cashew Chicken.

He walked up to 15th and to the restaurant closest to his apartment that had what he wanted. He was the only customer. It was that kind of a drizzly Wednesday night. When he entered, all of the cooks and waiters were sitting and laughing amongst themselves at a booth in the corner. They all stood when he entered and returned to their stations.

Jack ordered a Michelob and some food to go. It felt like a good night to be at home, but after a few refreshing swallows, he told the staff he intended to stay. The restaurant was warm. The fish tanks were reassuring, and it was strangely pleasant for him to be the only customer. He read the newspaper and was tempted to believe that a beer had never tasted so good as that particular beer tasted then and that every bite of Cashew Chicken was like a first kiss.

ALL DESIRE IS ABOUT FOREVER

Jack Waste wrote, "I can walk down the street and everyone knows my name but when I take my desire into account, all previously known definitions have to be redefined. It takes a long time to get over heartbreak. It takes a long time to sandbag the holes of doubt. One is less desirous in the cathedral of desire after being in the desert for so long. For a moment today I felt that everything was lost, but in that moment my desire was reinvented. Everyone's desire needs a desirous outlet. I desire a ship with a course set for the stars.

Disembodiment: allowing the eye to witness our alien existence as if it were not as familiar as we pretend it to be. Everything attempts to make us believe it *makes sense*, but how can we claim that anything *really* "make sense?"

We know it is time to leave the planet and its entertainments behind. Earth is not made of sand and coal, it is made of entertainment and poverty, bone and transmission. I need help understanding, especially my own hypocrisy, as I change the channel to more happy news.

The moon smiles and jets keep arriving from distant lands. Live your story. Time is escaping. The summer works against itself. Invest in the future. Winter isn't just an idea. There are heavy vibes in the air. Summer is ending. The quantum foam is depleted. Read your favorite poets and love the ones you love. The illusion of these times is being orchestrated *for* us, not *by* us. There *is* no shortage of creation, there *is* no downturn. To believe in propaganda is to suggest that we never had any power of belief to begin with. If one can overcome heartbreak then one can create one's own guest list to occupy the symphony hall of the mind.

The trade paperback trend of the sixties and seventies was the last glorious literary age of America. We need to bring it back. No one has yet to catch up to the new Golden Age. Few books, Nerval's excluded, were ever written by anyone who really understood the night. Perhaps a book needs to be written on *How To Be Unhappy* because everyone spends so much time trying to learn the opposite. How do spiders know how to spin webs? All I have are hundred dollar bills. This night could get interesting.

People walk slowly, weighed down by long faces and grocery bags. Of course, I too am a beggar of love. I wait for scraps, but still I am alive and well. I have my bottle of memories and will one day be an old man content to simply exist. The stars are smiling and will continue to smile long after we're gone.

I left the house in search of music and a crowd. At the corner, a woman stood with her face next to the side of a house as if she was reading it. I crossed over to the other side so as not to walk up behind her in the dark. She moved away from the house and stopped beneath the shadow of a tree. I could only see her hands in the streetlight. They were trembling.

On the main boulevard, workers were taking down the carnival tents. A street sweeper swept cigarette butts into his bin. Two women spoke French to each other as they strolled. A cool wind blew between the buildings and scattered leaves and debris. I was a ghost. At another corner, a woman stood examining a handful of green fuzz in one hand as she removed another handful from her pocket with her other hand. One bar was nearly empty. In another, a small shark swam in a tank above the bartender's head. I felt empty. No one knew my name. I started to head home.

What had I been looking for? Music and a crowd. I found neither, though from one store the mystical sounds of a faraway land tumbled from a speaker mounted to the wall. Life was far away even though life was all around. A Hungarian woman took me in just when I had given up on the night. She told me about her turtle that had wandered off and never returned. I pictured it out there somewhere in the empty soundless night. I walked home through streetlight shadows doing my best Robert De Niro walk to ward off night criminals. My blanket and sheets were warm in the dryer. I ate pizza and thought of the past. I ate pizza and thought of music and crowds.

DISSONANCE

There was a dissonance in the air. Jack Waste did not want to think that he was the only one feeling it because that would mean the ruin of his theory that there was something in the air. He noticed a change in the atmosphere in the early afternoon, when he started to feel heavy and sluggish. Was it the low-pressure system that had moved in? He looked outside the window at the city covered with a dense, low-hanging layer of fog and misting rain. The Space Needle appeared to be either out of focus, emerging from a cloud of smoke, or painted on canvas by Gerhard Richter.

Compacted into the next two hours, he: saw a police car pull someone over for a traffic violation, people staring into space at a coffee shop, rush hour bus windows filled with tired faces, his apartment door; took a ten minute nap with his shoes on after briefly staring at the ceiling; quietly walked the back streets towards 15th; drank a beer on a stool in The Canterbury reading short stories by Dylan Thomas; wandered back down the hill wondering where to go next; drank a poorly-made cocktail in a plastic cup at a new bar that had just opened and listened to an efficient but shapeless first three songs of a band with two guitarists who played the same chords and notes for every one of their songs while a young woman complained, "It's too LOUD!" Jack knew it was a hopeless night.

He was eager to get a snack and go home to bed. The Chinese restaurant near the end of Broadway was still open, but when the host approached, Jack could see he had a harried look in his eyes that said he just wanted to get the night over with. The waitress and chef were standing side by side and gave Jack a scornful look when he arrived. Jack was hungry and unswayed.

"Where is the love in Seattle?" he wondered. "Where is the love?"

There was an especially aggressive tone to the chopping and stir-frying as the chef took out his annoyance at having to churn out one last plate for an idiot off the street. The waitress said it had been a weird night and that she was glad it was almost over. As Jack walked down Broadway anchored by the weight of his takeout bag, he briefly looked up at the sky and a man walking almost next to him looked up too.

"Did you see something?" the guy asked.

"No, just looking," Jack said. The man, as they walked next to each other for two blocks, went on to recount stories of memorable comets he had seen in his lifetime.

"Have you ever *heard* one?" he asked. Jack shook his head. He had never thought it was possible to *hear* a comet.

"I heard one once. It was low," the man said, making his version of the falling comet's sound with pursed lips that sounded like a combination of a hiss and a whistle.

This small conversation about the universe's giddy dance was the reward for making it through a day of dissonance, Jack thought. The man said good night and crossed the street in the direction of the rest of his life.

As Jack walked up the final hill to his street to leave the day behind, he thought, "Capitol Hill, you have never surprised me."

When he turned the corner, a man pulled a tire from the back of a van, walked out into the center of the street, and to the amusement of his two friends, spun on his heels like a discus hurler and, with a loud guttural roar, launched the tire fifteen or twenty feet through the air. After it landed in the street with a loud "thop," the man picked up the tire and walked towards the building on the corner opposite to Jack's. He heard someone in the group say, "Did you get the six pack?" and pictured them drinking beer with a tire between them on the floor.

Jack turned the key, went inside, opened a beer, and gorged himself on string beans, pea pods, and garlic chicken like the wild dissonant beast he was until his belly told him "no more," after which he realized it was okay to say good night to the day and lay his head down to sleep.

FLOWERS UNDER CLOUDS

You were a rush hour number 7 bus down Broadway. You were a transfer in my pocket that meant I could get back. You were setting out from one place to get to another. I was tired and wanted to stay home but you called me out. You were the sudden opening up of the world while crossing Lake Union past memories of Kalakala sunsets, fireworks, boats trailing azure wakes, Mount Rainier on clear days, and sensations of descent into U-District wanderings, bookstores, faces, possibility.

You were a comfortable couch and a half nap in Café Roma surrounded by studying undergrads believing in their books. You were a closed off Ave. under reconstruction and slow-moving ghost-shapes of people moving slowly in the five o'clock bustle. You were the guy mopping the floor in slow motion at Flowers, the artist outside selling paintings done in hues of violet and red and pinks made translucent by the terror twilight. You were a chill in the air and a bar with no mood as me and Tabetha sat and talked about the nothingness of the day and the emptiness of the closed off street and the idea that perhaps it would be good to always have the Ave. closed like that so people could wander freely. You were a pint of pale ale on the bar and feeling dizzy from hunger and the rocking of the crowded bus. The pale ale lended its mood and a few people entered the bar, two couples on dates, one looking comfortable with each other, the other talking and laughing nervously while another young woman studied alone and took notes with a gin and tonic in hand.

Candles were lit but outside the street was still gray and people were cold and hunched over as they leaned into their nights. You were the pint glass ring I ran my fingers through on the counter. You were an inch of beer left in the glass. You were the hunger for something more. You were the evasion of chill and cloud and rain, the dream of soup and warmth and light. You were one couple leaving the bar and another one coming in. You were me and Tabetha leaving to go to the Ann Charters lecture and stopping for a slice of pizza on the way with Joe Strummer singing "Straight To Hell" as we ate. I saw him sing it a year earlier at The Showbox and wanted to hear it again since he died a few weeks earlier. Now it was part of the soundtrack to the night. You were the guy with an unhooked phone and dangling cords in hand and not enough money begging the pizza guys to forgive him being fifty-six cents short the prayer of a slice. You were another guy standing on the street eating his slice while staring down the street, a look of blank contentment in his eyes.

You were this slow accumulation of characters and moments, evidence of the hidden life of a city with no obvious reassuring hustle and bustle like New York, San Francisco, Boston, and Paris. You were empty moments, empty streets, gray skies, and rain. You were the hint of expectation on campus and ghosts moving towards words and knowledge and new faces in a lecture hall waiting expectantly to learn something new and now the lecture beginning and slowly unwinding memories of the past and how they fit into today's scheme of things.

You were always a city of should haves and could have beens and what I would love to be doing if I were somewhere else, only then to be humbled by the hidden moments that kept arriving despite all hope being lost at the thought that they might never return, despite the evidence that they always *did* return. You were the crusty old cab driver who drove us home complaining that Seattle women didn't flirt enough and telling stories of a wild date he had with a woman he met through a Stranger ad years earlier as his cab barely made it up the hill to Broadway and The Deluxe. You were the two of us wanting to keep the good vibe going so we crossed the street to Siam where you were broccoli tofu while sitting at the counter watching the beautiful women cook and feeling the warmth of the stoves on our faces.

You were the punk rocker standing on Broadway and John waiting to clean the windows of cars stopped at red lights for a handout. You were the graffiti tagger who stopped at every post to apply a tag who paused in the middle of his work to explain tagger aesthetics and styles and free walls and crews and getting into trouble for tagging a wall he thought was free but wasn't. You were a handshake, thanks bro, and a tagger continuing off into his night of tagging as I went home to bed and sleep with the thought that there aren't enough free walls in this town, that there needs to be more free walls. Free the walls, this town should live!

STRANGE BLANKET

There was a strange blanket over everything. Jack Waste had given up on finding anything resembling what he thought he was looking for. The streets were filled with people out and about, which made him feel a certain compulsion to be out and about amongst people too. It was Friday night. An obviously deranged cold front had set its vice-like grip over the city just when it seemed like spring was beginning to arrive. It was colder than it had been all winter. Even with enough layers to keep him warm, he found himself shivering. It was a fearful chill. There was talk of imminent war in the air. The terror alert had been raised to level orange. Life went on.

Jack decided at some point that his research about the night was telling him to go home and get some work done. Better to write something or play some music than to spend his little money in pursuit of a euphoria that wasn't in the air to be pursued. The night was a strange blanket.

As he walked, he looked up and saw a woman in a black robe light a cigarette on a balcony eight stories above the street. She was quite far away but against the low clouds of the night sky, her image was striking. She lit her cigarette, inhaled, and wrapped her arms around herself in a tight hug against the chill. A television's glow filled the room behind her. She took a second drag from her cigarette and crouched down so that her robe covered her knees. He wished he was on the other side of the sliding door, waiting for her to come back in from the cold. She looked down at him as he passed beneath the streetlights. He shivered and walked towards home, where only his bed waited to keep him warm.

SUPER BOWL SUNDAY EVE

The part of the world's population that did not care it was Super Bowl Sunday Eve went about its business on what was for them just another Saturday night. The part of the world's population that did care about the Super Bowl also went about its business, but with one difference: they were looking forward to the spectacle of the game. For this part of the population, Super Bowl Sunday was a national holiday.

Jack Waste lay on his bed listening to the rain. It was the kind of slow steady Seattle rain that caused time to slow down to a stop. If you had a lover during this kind of rain, it made you feel like there would be no end to your existence together. Those without lovers lay in beds all over the city wrestling with unpleasant thoughts of unmet desire.

He rose late with no real agenda to get much done except to go music shopping, eat, rest, and dream. He left his apartment a little bit before three o'clock in the afternoon.

The world had started around him and seemed to be going about its business with little difficulty. He bought two records and walked a few blocks down Broadway before realizing he had no more reason to be out in the world that afternoon.

He stopped at the supermarket, where he bought salmon for dinner. After he ate, he lay down and watched the light turn from grey to the lightest version of cobalt blue that one rarely saw in any other medium but reality. Few cinematographers were able to capture the nuances of this kind of light and few painters or photographers stood a chance of translating this rare hue with their own art forms. It lingered as if it was something solid and then was suddenly gone.

Jack closed his shades and napped for an hour. When he woke, it was completely dark outside and the world felt far away, if it still existed at all. He ran through his mind all the different places he could go if he wanted to go out but none of them called his name, so he decided to stay home. After some more time had passed, though, he realized he was getting hungry again and decided to walk back down to Broadway for a plate of nachos.

The first thing he saw outside was a guy and a girl trying to push their car out onto a hill so they could get it jump started. Jack offered his assistance and helped get the car rolling. The couple thanked him and moved on into their future.

Next he saw a man and woman talking in front of the Mystery Soda machine next to the key shop on John. The machine had four flavors of soda to purchase plus a Mystery Flavor, which was never the same. Once, Jack stood there with a friend and bought seven Mystery Flavors in a row. Each time, the flavor was different. Jack thought the machine was one of the wonders of Capitol Hill.

As he passed, the man put in the necessary coins, pressed the Mystery Flavor button, and said excitedly when the can came out of the machine, "see, it's always different." Jack was pleased to learn there were other Mystery Flavor aficionados in the world.

When he turned the corner at Broadway, he saw a guy walking slowly down the sidewalk with his girlfriend sitting on his shoulders. Jack watched as they waited for a light to change, then crossed the street and continued on west into the neighborhood.

He took a table at La Cocina and ordered a beer and a plate of nachos. A couple was seated two tables away. As Jack read a story from his Dylan Thomas book, he listened as they quietly argued. He could not hear what the man was saying, but every time he spoke her response was a variation of, "I can do whatever I want to do and you have to respect that. You can't tell me what I can and cannot do. I'm tired of men telling me what I can and cannot do." Based on the tone of their conversation, Jack couldn't see why they were even bothering to sit with each other, and felt satisfied that he wasn't in a relationship that might take that kind of turn on an otherwise peaceful Saturday night.

Jack finished his nachos, paid his check, and decided to buy a can of beer and head home. As he approached the supermarket he noticed a very drunk woman wearing high heels veering back and forth as she walked towards the supermarket. After he selected his can of beer, he walked past an aisle and watched as the woman teetered and opened a bottle of olive oil. After the cap slipped from her hand, she stood with the bottle at her nose and sniffed it for several long seconds. He watched as she crouched and nearly fell while picking up the cap, which she then replaced on the bottle and put back on the shelf, then chose a different brand to open and smell.

When he left the supermarket, he looked back and saw her in line, pulling wadded bills from a pocket and placing them in a pile on the counter.

On the corner diagonal to the market, two young women leaned over their male friend, who was seated on the curb and almost passed out between his own legs. They tried to lift him up and get him to his feet while complaining bitterly to each other about the rain. With some effort, they managed to get him moving down the sidewalk. He was in a terrible condition, far beyond drunken bliss. It would be a long Super Bowl Sunday for him unless he possessed the fortitude that allowed some partiers to wake up as if nothing had happened to their bodies the night before.

Now, laying in his bed listening to the rain and the sound of train horns baying into the night, Jack felt the world hold its breath and made a wish for better days to come, for long rainy Saturday afternoons and nights in the arms of a suitable lover.

Further away, in San Diego, each member of the teams that were going to play in the Super Bowl either lay restlessly awake waiting for the sun to rise with the hope of possible victory on their minds or slept the sound sleep of warriors not concerned about what would happen on the battlefield the next day.

The football field itself lay stretched out beneath the night sky and universe above and even further away, far across time, where the members of a civilization on another planet that had yet to be discovered sighed and slept and went about their own business on a world with different names for everything we have names for on our own.

Outside his window, a man and woman's footsteps passed through the night. Jack closed his eyes and waited for sleep.

SOMETHING OUT OF NOTHING

Walking down Broadway, Jack Waste enjoyed the poetry of everything in motion. Everything seemed to be part of a choreographed painting. An absurdly huge drilling mechanism painted bright sky blue rolled slowly down the street on the back of a trailer. It dwarfed everything on the street and made him feel like a miniature person in an architect's model.

The sun was out and it was beginning to resemble summer again after a week of false rain and cold had set things back a season. The rain had come at the height of desire and possibility and clamped down on the heat-filled nights of sweat and flesh. Just when everyone had accepted the fact that the heat was there to stay, it had gone away. He could see in everyone's eyes that they had withdrawn to whatever place in their minds was reserved for the gray weather, and he felt it too.

As he crossed the street towards Angel's Thai restaurant he pondered the temptation to have lunch sitting in a window seat so he could stare out at the street. He reminded himself of his financial situation, though, and decided that it would be best to make lunch at home and save his money for a near-future night out on the town. He sat on the bus stop bench near Angel's and idled for a while to figure out his next move.

The sun felt good on his face. Dance music blared from the store behind him and provided a soundtrack, though perhaps a false soundtrack, for the day. A cycle of time passed. Three buses came and went. He did not want to appear to be an idler, even though he was happy to sometimes be, as Dylan Thomas put it in his short story "Just Like Little Dogs," "a steady stander-at-corners."

He read two poems from the collection of Pablo Neruda's work he was carrying with him. In the first, "And How Long?," Neruda wrote, "How much does a man live, after all? Does he live a thousand days, or one only? What does it mean to say 'forever?' Lost in this preoccupation, I set to clear things up."

The poet goes in search of answers from people he thinks should know, priests and doctors, but no one is able to satisfy his questions about existence, even the gravediggers, and he is finally told to "get yourself a good woman and give up this nonsense." The poem ends with the poet writing, "I returned home, much older after crossing the world. Now I ask questions of nobody. But I know less every day."

"I know less every day." Jack repeated the line in his head and thought about what it meant. There were days he felt like he knew nothing and that everyone was pretending to know the things they appeared to think they knew. He waited a few minutes for his eyes to adjust from the glare of the sun's reflection off the pages of the book, then read a second poem, "Fable Of The Mermaid And The Drunks."

It was a very strange poem about a mermaid who came from a river and arrived, beautiful, mysterious and naked, in a bar filled with drunks. The men spat at her and hurled obscenities her way. "She was a mermaid who had lost her way," Neruda wrote. Jack did not understand why the men did not welcome the mermaid who had lost her way. If he were ever in a bar and a mermaid walked in, he would certainly welcome her.

"Her eyes were the color of faraway love." That line made him stop and think for a moment. He tried to picture eyes the color of faraway love and wanted to meet such a woman. The mermaid eventually leaves the bar and returns to the river, where "she was cleansed, gleaming once more like a white stone in the rain; and without a backward look, she swam once more, swam towards nothingness, swam to her dying."

Jack did not understand this fable, but he felt a longing for the mermaid with eyes "the color of faraway love." He closed his book and looked at the people wandering up and down Broadway. He had stayed too long.

The moon looked down and saw that a slew of possible moments had arrived below and passed by untendered. As it slipped below the horizon, no one saw it shed a tear of grief that fell into the Sea Of Tranquility. The sun noticed, but by then it too had started its descent as Jack's side of the Earth continued its solo passage through madness and time.

HICCUP OF DESIRE

Jack Waste wrote, "I know my desire means nothing in the grand scheme of the universe. That is not to say that it means nothing in the grand scheme of the universe of my existence. Therefore, *perhaps* my desire means *something* in the grand scheme of the universe.

Say the progeny of my desire were to eventually grandfather and grandmother itself down twelve generations hence. Some of those progeny would go on to travel out into the nether regions of space. Would they be as workers on a cruise ship or poets exploring the unknown and reporting back their findings via music, art, and metaphor?

I would hope for the latter as all I really want myself right now is a spaceship filled with fuel, food, music, beer, pens, and blank notebooks. I would like nothing better than to be shot out into space with the facilities to keep myself alive and living the relatively tame but wild existence I am living now, albeit in space from where I would report back to Earth my weekly findings.

It's a despicable thought that most of our fellow Earthlings feel little pull towards outer space. Perhaps we have only our best scientists to blame, or their administrators who have no sense of the poetic and only think in terms of tangibles. Send some of us impractical folk out there! When I head out into the night knowing from the get go that I am not going to travel farther than my immediate neighborhood and its trajectory of restaurants and bars, I have no idea what I am going to encounter. This fact exhilarates me. Space travel is no different.

Like tonight, St. Valentine's Day: why did I leave the house only to be repelled by everything the universe threw my way? My only plan: visit five art galleries having openings from six to nine p.m. in my immediate neighborhood. The plan was to head out into the night with an anthropological ally. It being Valentine's Day, though, allies were in short supply. Everyone I knew seemed to have sickeningly specific plans that were set in stone.

The night was a slaughter right from the start. As you read this you should be able to feel the palpable *nothingness* in the air outside the window. It is an oppressive feeling, but the more I write the more I feel that I am the only one in the city who is really alive, and this notion emboldens me in my effort the more I continue on with my thoughts.

The first gallery I encountered was sparsely encountered. I had started out too early, but then I was not interested in going inside as there was no evidence of wildness unless it was purely verbal and lip. There appeared to be no passage of food and wine, no circumference of desire. It was very sterile. Is this the NEW ART?

Many galleries feel like management training meetings or ORIENTATION DISCOS. Things weren't always this way. Where is THE DANGER? That being said, I wasn't looking for trouble, only a substitute for the absence of fun. One look inside said it was just the gallery owner and their friends. Where's the fun in that? Art is not insular. We are beaten down.

Can I have some of your french fries?

I pondered entering a bar and leaving the art galleries behind, but realized that I wanted to go no further. Everyone out was a couple. I saw red heart balloons everywhere.

And to think that I had set out so innocently...

I had wanted to learn a universal language. I had wanted to return home at the end of the night to write about art and desire. This lit is not it.

There needs to be more surrender. There needs to be more resistance. SURRENDER: to the reckless abandon of meeting new strangers, consequences be damned and embraced as normal aberrations in the weeks to follow. RESISTANCE to all that impedes surrender.

Maybe I'm just talking to myself. If so, and you see me on the street, say hello and stop me, stop me, stop me.

HOW TO BE MINDFUL

Life is life and death. Every moment has the capacity to be epic or pathetic. You don't need to know what you already know, but it keeps rearing its head to remind you. The seduction of entertainment is enough to transcend everything. Wounds heal. Scars remain to tell their stories.

Jack Waste stood on Broadway drinking water next to a garbage can after picking up a cane from the pharmacy. A very light rain was falling. Jack Waste felt dizzy and weak. He had limped from the doctor's office after he gave him the okay to walk on his injured knee. Walk is the wrong word. He had to wear an ankle to thigh stabilizer for the next eight weeks to keep his leg straight. The effort of walking was exhausting. He finished his water, threw the empty bottle in the garbage, and hobbled over to the crosswalk to wait for the light to change. A twenty-something woman stood near him at the crosswalk waiting for the light to change. She had a book in her hand: *How To Be Mindful*. Ha. Maybe he should have read it before he crashed his bike.

The light changed and they stepped into the crosswalk. She reached the other side of the street when Jack was just reaching the halfway point. She continued walking down Broadway and Jack continued up the hill towards his apartment, where he fell on his bed and closed his eyes.

How To Be Mindful. You can take the clues thrown your way each day in two ways: as lessons or as leavings. Sometimes they are lessons after the fact. Jack closed his eyes for what he thought would be a short nap and woke up five hours later. His body was telling him to rest. It was a hard thing to accept. There was much to do but life was life and death. He turned on his television. They were showing footage of the attacks on the World Trade Center two years earlier. Be mindful. Every day is 9/11.

THE BED OF MEMORY

SHED YOUR CONTAINERS!

Everything moves too fast. Party while you can, there will be no more parties one day, only memories and you, frozen in time, dancing, laughing, surrounded by friends, immortal together forever, safe and alive in time, in the night, the endless party, party night.

THE CIBSTRYCTION OF DRINKS

It's a Jack Waste Sunday night. One weekend's worth of memories weigh in against the setting sun's long shadows. A quick happy hour schooner, then home for salmon, wasabi mashed potatoes, and asparagus for dinner, a little Sunday night television, a movie, some sounds played on the bass, then sleep and dreams.

12XU. The Wire show at the Showbox the night before had passed in a hyperspace eye blink of euphoric rhythm and sound. It was much too short and had left Jack wanting more. Colin Newman was out of his mind, a mad look in his eyes, come to Seattle as a wake-up call to action and musical arms.

Jack's two basses leaning in the corner and the drum set in the other room were enough of a cache to lead a small band into the din of the beehive.

Jack felt like writing. He put his coaster on top of his glass and walked across Broadway from Ileen's to the convenience store at the corner to buy a pad of paper. The woman on line in front of him was buying five lollipops.

"I like sour," she said to the cashier. "You don't like sour?"

The cashier crinkled up his nose and said, "No, I like sweet."

Jack paid for his pad of paper and walked back towards the bar. A shifty-looking guy zig-zagging down the sidewalk zagged past him and muttered under his breath, "Smoke weed, dude?"

His beer sat waiting for him where he'd left it. Smoke from the bartender's cigarette rose like a column into the shadows of the ceiling. Psychedelic colors bounced and refracted off the bottles behind the bar.

Jack scribbled some lines in his notebook until he finished his beer and walked home in the rain. He felt like an outcast. Even the cab drivers asked for directions.

Video games, multiplexes, what a terrible world. The only beauty was "raindrops keep falling on my head." Everything was *institutionalized*. Butch and Sundance duking it out to the end gave him hope.

"F.B.I., man," someone said when he walked by, insulting Jack as he wrote in his notebook in the rain. He must have looked "official" in his blue jacket.

"F.B.I.?" he thought, tempted to yell, "*Internet*, you fucker!"

It seemed to Jack that time was going by faster than it used to. He wondered if anyone else felt restless and disjointed. He wondered how many other people felt time moving faster. Time was out of control and nobody was at the wheel.

Jack Waste leaned over his notebook and wrote, "We forget to remember we are hurtling through space. We argue and fight over little things. We break each other's hearts instead of holding on.

Here I am on Planet Earth. Will I never get off this rock and make it out into the stars? We act like television is real and that we are going to live forever.

We forget to talk to the stranger sitting next to us in the park while the crickets chirp and the stars spin their infinite web of stories in the sky.

Tonight he was alive in the great machine of the universe. Tomorrow would be another day on Earth. There was nothing to go back to, only the present and future, from which the past returned every now and then as a reminder of all that was and all that will be The Big Everything."

PLEASURES

Hostess Snowballs, candlelight, moonlight, sunlight, red light, blue eyes, green eyes, gray eyes, brown eyes, Jalapeno Poppers, hugging, kissing, the Sunday paper, Hefeweizen with lemon in the summer, taxi cab rides home from downtown, being in a trance state, Italian food, Mexican food, Thai food, cooking magazines, silver dollar pancakes, being awake at three in the morning, cool breezes, swinging in a hammock, swinging on a porch swing, Sunday brunch, the Sonics on TV in the rainy season, pay day, scratch lottery tickets, warm laundry just out of the dryer, movie previews, afternoon naps, waiting for the bus, mailing a package to a friend, chips and salsa, airplane food, the Space Needle, reading in bed, accidental spectacular pool shots, the view of Earth from space, New York City, Paris, Brussels, Los Angeles, Boston, letters from overseas, tacos, ice cold beer on hot summer days, reading the newspaper, spring rolls, chewing gum, pillows, a favorite pen, bookstore cats, running into people you know, smiles from strangers, walking under an umbrella, finding money on the ground, marshmallows, grocery lists...

HEFEWEIZEN

The first Hefeweizen of the season reminded Jack Waste that summer was on the horizon. It was late April. There was just a hint of summer in the air, just a hint of heat. It was an illusion, of course. There were still some winter rainy nights and wind blowing over the hill ahead, but this first Hefeweizen of the season reminded him of the languorous days and nights to come: jukebox change on the table at Ileen's, a couple of laughing friends, pitchers of Hefeweizen (Widmer, only Widmer), lemons floating on top, and the Sonics on TV, deep in the playoffs, making a run.

LAST CALL

Jack Waste was walking home one night after mingling with humanity at a club down the street. There had been much music and dancing and a good time seemed to be had by all. Jack had not met anyone new nor even found anyone to talk to, but he had fulfilled his goal of going out and having at least a semblance of a night out on the town.

As he walked home in the shadows of the trees on Eleventh, he passed a house from which he could hear a party going on. He walked up onto the yard between the house and the building next door to see if there was evidence that it might be an open party he would be welcome to enter.

As he contemplated his next move, he heard a cough from the window of the building next to the party house. He looked to his left just as the lights in the room went on. It was a home for the elderly. There were four beds in the room, one in each corner, and in each was a frail old woman. One of them opened her eyes and watched as the nurse turned one of the other women onto her side.

Jack looked over his shoulder at the party next door and tried to imagine the parties the ladies had attended in their day. He sighed and walked quietly down the street and up the hill to his apartment, where he climbed into bed and left the night behind.

He looked forward to his next night out, eager to raise his glass in toast to the frail old angels asleep in their beds of memory.

THE WINE STORIES

TREES

On his Saturday afternoon walk around Capitol Hill, Jack Waste noticed dead Christmas trees everywhere. It was the sixth weekend after Christmas and people were just now getting rid of them. He didn't remember ever seeing Christmas trees put out on the curb so long after the holidays and wondered if the attack on the World Trade Center towers in September had anything to do with people holding onto something that gave them comfort longer than usual.

Most of them appeared to have been well taken care of and didn't have the dried up look that most discarded trees had in previous seasons. If he had thought to count the number of trees he saw, he would guess that he had walked by at least fifty. They appeared on every block. Sometimes two or three were stacked against each other like bodies of people who had been shot by either an advancing or retreating army.

Even though he knew each one was dead the moment it had been cut down and taken for sale to some tree lot far from where it had spent several peaceful years waiting to reach harvest age, Jack felt like a Christmas tree was only truly dead when it was finally discarded and had ceased to fulfill the purpose of its existence. It seemed sad that their only purpose was to one day be tossed out onto the street, but then, their fate only mirrored everything else's fate in the world, so perhaps that was what compelled Jack to empathize with their demise.

What could be done? Nothing could stop the march of time. He couldn't get out of his mind the images of bodies of people killed during wartime when he looked at the trees strewn everywhere. He pictured a pasture in which people had been planted and grew from the ground, only to be uprooted and relocated for a few weeks in the homes of those who had come to choose them before being put out on the street when their time of usefulness had ended. He wanted to take each tree home and give it a new life or think of another way to put the trees to use after they had become an eyesore to their owners.

The congregation of the church next to his apartment building had attempted to sell Christmas trees that year, but from all appearances, it had not been much of a success. Three weeks after Christmas, the lot was filled with over a hundred trees. When Jack walked home at night, he thought of taking one in and decorating it even though the holiday season was over.

One morning when he woke up he heard the sound of a wood chipper and when he left his building he saw that they were chopping up all the Christmas trees that hadn't been sold.

Later in the night, when he was returning home from work, Jack smelled the fresh scent of the chopped up evergreens. It hung in the air at his corner as a reminder of primitive forest powers. It didn't matter that the smell of an evergreen reminded Jack of Christmases past; there was something else the smell suggested, something *older*, further back in time. Had his distant ancestors in the caves also derived pleasure from the smell of pines?

A week or so after the church ground up their leftover Christmas trees, Jack noticed they had spread the cuttings on top of the dirt around the parking lot as compost. He stood next to the remaining pile of ground-up evergreens and inhaled its scent.

The rain fell as a mist that no umbrella could defend. It was not a day to be alone and yet there were people alone all over the city trying to stay warm and ward off the awareness that they were alone, trying to ignore the fact that someone unmet who might remedy their sense of isolation was either just across town or in another town on the other side of the world. Who really knows if they are in the right place at the right time?

If given the choice, would a tree ask to be ground up and planted as mulch to enable a future something to grow or would it ask to stand shivering with its fellow brethren in the woods for the duration of its natural life? Would the trees want us to feel sad at the sight of them laying near the curb, waiting to be picked up by the garbage man, or would they want us to feel happy at having fulfilled their purpose in such a spectacular manner with the time they were allowed?

Jack shivered, shook his head in confusion, and continued on down the street. One day soon it will be summer again, he thought, and none of this will make sense.

CRIME

When Ileen's was still open, Jack sometimes stood on line at the bank across the street waiting to make a deposit and imagined handing the teller a note asking for all the money in the till. He knew it wouldn't be much, but he also knew he would take the sack across the street and buy everyone who happened to be seated at the bar a round of drinks.

He pictured himself feeding dollar bill after dollar bill into the jukebox and then sitting calmly in the window with a pitcher of Hefeweizen as the police arrived. He knew it would get ugly soon after and that he would probably find himself holed up in the men's room with a bottle of whiskey, thinking about the good times of his life and reading from the pages of the strange paperbacks pasted onto the walls as the SWAT team moved in with tear gas and concussion grenades.

Jack was partial to tunnel jobs. His favorite heist story was about a tunnel job that went down in Paris in the late seventies. Not only did the robbers make off with millions of dollars and the contents of safety deposit boxes, they also took the time to cook and eat a meal in the confines of the vault, wine included. Those thieves had true style and a job like that took real imagination. They were artists through and through. Jack had never begun the apprenticeship that would lead him to pull of a big tunnel heist one day. He was just another petty dreamer dreaming of the heist that would one day set him free.

THE NIGHT

Jack Waste wrote, "The night sighed and I sighed with it. I left everything to chance and chance left everything up to me. By chance, I saw a woman dancing in her window when I walked by on my way to the store. By chance, I heard one hustler explain a hustle to another hustler on the bus. By chance I saw three people share a laugh in the window of the teriyaki shop. With chance, everything is free.

Someday I'll finally make up my mind, you'll see, but tonight, something broke and let out its long-saved breath. Does this mean it is safe to go out? Does this mean I'd find a lover to hold my hand? Or would I be a sucker to my own state of calm and find that I am the night's closed mouth that didn't exhale, and that everything is grime and gas?

Tonight at midnight, I sat on the bed reading Khlebnikov and found I wasn't as alone as I thought. The sun came out but I missed the rain. I even missed the lonely train. Should I go out? What would I find, the path back after the passage of time? It's one a.m. bar time, what would that get me? I've only got a few dollars left until payday, should I save them for tomorrow or throw them away?

No one will ever know what I did this night. I am a stranger sitting alone in a room and even though I'm pretending I'm satisfied to stay in for the rest of the night, I've got a pretty good mind to meet a strange woman and bring her home for pancakes and chess. Lately, though, someone's been forgetting to tell the strange women it's safe to come out. It's a terrible year for the imagination, everyone so grounded in this thing of reality. Where's the absurdity?"

Jack capped his pen and sighed. Writing had made his brain sing and dance a little bit, but now he found himself craving the promise every night suggested when unmet desire made itself known like a lighthouse glimpsed for the first time from the bow of a ship in the midst of a long journey. The night was a living room. Everything was peaceful and in its place and there was a gentleness in the air like a smooth coat of paint. The neighborhood felt like an architect's model. There wasn't any activity in any of the homes. Everything was still.

Jack walked with a bottle of wine under his arm but never found the party he'd been invited to. The address given to him turned out to be the house of the first party in Seattle he went to long ago. Everything seemed far away and out of reach then. Everyone seemed to know each other and he didn't know anyone. Now his immediate world was a familiar room. He knew where everything was and instead of expecting the unexpected he now expected narrative flow, concision, and the continuation of what had come before.

He stood in front of the house at the end of Bellevue and remembered standing on the other side of its living room window that night years ago in another universe of time. He stood with his bottle of wine and stared at the nonexistent party. Only the blue of a television's glow filled the room. No party anywhere tonight, he thought. Somewhere someone was dying but for everyone else tonight there was only sleep and the fatigue that came with the knowledge that the battle with winter was over.

As he neared his apartment he heard explosions in the air and turned to see where they were coming from. They sounded like fireworks but nothing appeared in the sky. Two drunk guys and a drunk woman stumbled towards him.

"Did you hear those explosions?" Jack Waste asked.

"What explosions?" they answered in unison. Nobody knew anything. He walked home. A strange night, he thought. Tomorrow was Saturday.

A day of relaxation. A day of rest.

LET GO

Jack Waste wrote, "Let go, let go, there's nowhere to go. Stay up past midnight with a bottle of wine and wait for your thoughts to come. The day does everything to dull them; the night does everything to make you forget. Watch television, watch a movie, talk on the phone, send an e-mail. It's all just an outflowing of what should be flowing IN. What feeds you, the woman dancing in the window, dark shadows in alleys, or illumination by candlelight at midnight beneath the gray hush of clouds? After a false day of spring, winter has returned, not with a vengeance, but with the realization that its days are numbered.

I got nothin', O, I got nothin' but an appreciation for the EVERYTHING that has come before, and now that I've cultivated that appreciation, none of it makes any sense at all. At the same time, I'm not sure I have such a good idea about what tomorrow is supposed to bring and I'm sure I'm not the only person who feels this way.

How many nights like tonight can go by without a fundamental change? Forever trapped in the Stone Age, forever trapped in competition when there should only be an advance towards the stars. We know we're not going to stay on Earth forever, so let's go see what's out there.

I've been lonelier than lonely on this planet Earth and for the entire last year I could just as easily have traveled out into space and back and felt no worse for wear. I only need food and wine and something to write with. The question becomes one of sanity: can our long distance space travelers survive the lengthy trip? Given the proper support items, anyone can survive anything. Send us out there with pills, with booze, with virtual reality, with whatever inebriant or numbing manifestation of delusion or distraction we can come up with to help get us through the journey and we'll be just fine. Our problem is that we continue to believe in "Home Sweet Home." Let's go!

In the morning, the evening of the day before was still happening. It was raining and felt like every other morning felt when it was raining. Outside, a single construction worker in a rain suit appeared to be doing performance art rather than working. He lifted a piece of wood, tossed it to the side, hammered at a piece of cement, threw a stone from the pit to the sidewalk, stood back to look at his work, kicked a two by four away from the pit, wiped some grit from a cement platform. On television, the horror of morning rush hour traffic played out in a slow motion dance of red and white lights. Train horns sounded through the gray air. Everyone wished they were back in bed."

RED, RED WINE

Halfway through the last glass of what had been a nearly empty to begin with bottle of Washington State merlot, Jack Waste realized he should have bought a second bottle of wine when he was at the supermarket. Each bottle had its own soul and ability to reshape one's mood to resemble its vintage. Jack was just discovering the intricacies of these moods for the first time. He had tasted many wines over the years but never had the epiphany that made him see that wine was more than just the word used to name it. It was a bottle of Spanish red a few weeks earlier that had changed everything.

Had it just been his mood that evening that led to the epiphany? He wasn't sure. All he knew was that the bottle of Codice Tinto he'd seen featured in a supermarket ad for $6.99 had given him the greatest feeling of giddy joy he remembered having in years. Sitting at his computer working on a manuscript of old writings, he noticed that he was suddenly deep into the bottle when he had intended to have just a glass. He found himself grinning as he wrote and felt a warmth pulse through his body that he had never felt from wine before.

"This wine's got quite a mood," he thought.

A few days later, he bought a second bottle of the Codice Tinto. He wanted to find out if what he had felt from the first bottle was present in the second. Sure enough, half a slow bottle later while working on a manuscript at his computer, he felt the same happy glow wash over him. Where did it come from? What was in the wine that was making him feel this way? It had to be more than the alcohol. He'd enjoyed beer, mixed drinks, and other wine in years past, but none of them had ever contained a mood of such giddy joy. Inebriation, yes, but giddy joy? Never. He drank half the bottle, grinned broadly as he worked, and went to bed early, feeling how he imagined a happy man felt at the end of his day.

The next night, after finishing some mundane tasks that needed to be taken care of, he decided to have a glass. He had been in a bad mood previously, but sure enough, after a single glass he was flushed with a grin on his face and warmth in his bones, and just as suddenly as he realized he was suddenly in a suddenly giddy mood, the wine was gone.

He decided to walk to the supermarket closest to his apartment and get a bottle of wine. They didn't carry the Codice Tinto, though, and he didn't feel like walking the rest of the way to the other supermarket that had an ample supply on their shelves. He selected an inexpensive but elegantly named French red.

The whole world was liquid. He felt immortal and alive, a movie star, not in human form but the celluloid version that lived forever. He was floating above the linoleum floor. When he reached the checkout counter, the cashier took one look at him and smiled with a knowing look in her eyes.

"Anything else?" she asked.

"Yeah," he said, "A corkscrew." She laughed and handed him his change. Suddenly, the giddiness disappeared. Where a moment before he had been immortal he now felt like he was nothing, truly nothing. What had happened? The Codice Tinto had run out on him.

He walked home in the rain and opened the new bottle, but the French red did not have a mood. He knew then that he was hooked, that he had a vision of what wine could be, and he knew for sure there was a whole new realm of knowledge to seek out.

Jack loved to stand in front of the shelves of wine. It made him feel the same way he felt wandering among the library stacks on snowy winter afternoons when he was a grad student. He knew that each wine, like each book on the shelves, was a different mood, a different place, a different flavor and state of mind, and that each winemaker was the author of that mood. Instead of words and ink, the winemakers used grapes.

Staring at the wall of wine, Jack realized his responsibility as a writer was to create as tangible a mood with words as a good bottle of wine induced so that the experience in the reader's mind bordered on being a physical sensation and one close to inebriation."

Just as Jack Waste wrote this last line, the bottle of Washington State merlot he was working on gave way to its sad empty bottom. He sighed and realized that one more glass would make him feel right at home in the immensity of the cold winter night, so he put on his shoes and walked two blocks up to the 7-11, where they had an odd assortment of bottles on a rack next to the beer coolers. He chose an inexpensive merlot and waited on line to pay while reading a magazine article about a particularly fierce battle that had taken place a week earlier in Afghanistan.

He felt far away from "the world" as he walked back to his apartment. He knew there were clubs and bars filled with people, but he knew it was his turn to stay home and get some work done. Low clouds hung like a padded ceiling over the top of the hill. He turned the key in his door and, before taking off his coat, opened the bottle to let it breathe.

THE FUTURE OF OUR PAST
(SAY SOMETHING THAT WILL PLEASE ME)

Jack Waste wrote, "There has to be a way to unify those who are alive with those from our literary heritage who have died. I see pictures of Daumal, Rimbaud, Jarry, Desnos. Add any name to this list of those who stare back at us from the time of black and white daguerreotypes and we are sure to be left yearning for time travel. I see a look in some of their eyes that suggests they wanted to make it known that if time travel ever came to pass we should put them at the top of the list to make the trip.

What age, what year would you time travel to if you had the chance? Who amongst us would travel willingly into the past with the knowledge that we would die there even as our ideas would take hold and live forever in the literary future? Khlebnikov, Soupault, Artaud, Breton, Cravan, Roussel: these and all who they were associated with appear like they arrived from a future of unknown design. How would we ever know if time travel had become possible in the future of our past and that these literary visionaries were actually stranded and not citizens of those distant eras?

What writers of the present appear to be from the future? Who seems to be saying anything that is beyond our understanding? Who has time traveled to speak to us today? Are we worth talking to or are we a lost segment of history, an insignificant moment trapped between significant moments? Perhaps we are playing it *too* cool."

Jack Waste capped his pen. Was he a hungry satellite passing a lonely planet or a lonely planet yearning for a passing satellite? All past expectations had released Jack from feeling expectant. He was waiting for the river of stone to pass him by and release him from its grasp. Reality was not as wild and in flux as he needed it to be and so he tumbled and stumbled on. It was all he could do to keep himself from laughing out loud sometimes at the absurdity of it all. Things were red without passion. Things were red without red. He knew who he was but his surroundings did not.

Jack Waste wrote, "Let be those who will be. The rest of us, the restless, let's coagulate into some new organism. We recognize that third and fourth choices are needed. We like to believe that everyone is discovering new routes of adventure through creativity. No more institutions, commercial breaks, product placements, no more belief in old ideas, but instead only in something new that we have yet to design. Why isn't there more pressure to let our hearts throb NOW? We were on the brink in the very beginning. It was right there for us to embrace, but then we invented authority to shut it down, and since then we have only created *entertainment lessons*.

What about pure realization? Re-entry, zero-g, the possibility of life with altered gravity? Have we misread the signs? Why do we spend so much time trying to catch up with everything already done and seen? Where is the urgency? Why so much sitting around like penguins waiting to suffer their fate? We grew up with television and film as our reality. Generations before us were more rooted in the moment. Today's generations watch the future arrive".

Jack capped his pen and walked up to the store to get a snack. On his way back with a bag of chips, Jack noticed a man sitting on the ground next to a bush on the corner.

The man said, "I'm trying to find Jesus, brother."

Jack pulled five ones from his pocket and handed them to the man. "This is for Jesus," he said.

"Thank you, brother," the man said, taking the bills.

Jack looked over his shoulder as he walked towards his apartment. The man was still sitting there, watching Jack go.

"I love you too, brother," he said.

ROYAL PALMS

Jack Waste was tired and thought of staying in but on television a forty-one year old linesman won Game Three of the Stanley Cup with a shot in triple overtime and made Jack think he had more than enough gas to go see forty-four year old Mike Watt play at The Crocodile, and so he headed out into the night.

As he walked downtown, Jack's mind wandered back to sunsets near the Pacific, where he once lived a few miles up the coast from Mike Watt's town of San Pedro. His room faced west. Each sunset was a unique show of light and sound as the foghorns of passing ships echoed and whales passed by in winter while waves crashed against the shipwreck shores at the base of the cliffs.

Sometimes he stood on the hill behind his house and took it all in: the Pacific, Catalina Island, the far horizon. Love and everything else were still just book dreams of an imagined future. Skateboarding down the hill to school, though, was real.

1980-1983. High school. *Apocalypse Now, Star Wars, The Empire Strikes Back*, Pink Floyd's *The Wall*, U2's *Boy, October*, and *War*, O.M.D.'s first three albums, and a daily dose of New Wave on KROQ were the weft of Jack's early soundtrack weave.

Hearing New Order's *Power, Corruption, And Lies* played in its entirety at one in the morning on a Los Angeles college radio station made Jack aware of the world beyond his window.

He felt restless to explore it as he weeded yards while listening to the repeating daily grind of 80's hits that people now think of as "classics." Punk rock would arrive for Jack after New Wave, after he'd graduated high school and finally gone out into the world, where Black Flag and The Minutemen waited to greet him.

In 1985, Jack saw the Minutemen, The Ramones, and Black Flag on the same bill at the Hollywood Palladium. Punks outside rioted after the show was declared sold out. As Jack and his friends left afterwards, helicopters circled overhead while riot police ran after punks with clubs raised high through tear gas clouds.

Jack noted that the scene was just like a similar sequence in Pink Floyd's *The Wall*. As they pulled out of the parking lot, they watched in amazement as Belinda Carlisle of the Go-Go's emerged in slow motion from a back door of the club and stepped into the midst of the chaos.

As Jack walked through the club looking for his friends, Jack thought about the last time he saw Mike Watt play fourteen years earlier. Jack lived in Brussels for a year and when he saw that firehose, Watt's new band following the death of his Minutemen band mate and friend D. Boon, was coming to play at the Ancienne Belgique, he and his brother, both homesick for Los Angeles, went to the show.

They ended up drinking beer and talking with Watt for an hour at a table in the lounge outside the venue's main room while the opening band Crime And The City Solution played. It turned out that Watt was also homesick for Los Angeles and so they spent a lot of the time talking about San Pedro and the South Bay and the Lakers playing in the finals against the Pistons.

After his third beer, Watt went off on a buzzed tangent about the brilliance of James Joyce's poetry in *Ulysses* while punks in leather jackets climbed through the second story barred windows of the club from the alley below.

During the show, Jack and his brother sat on the band's equipment cases to the side of the small stage. Mike Watt's fingers bled as he played and later Jack and his brother took the tram home out of their minds from the adrenaline rush of the show.

Though his fingers didn't bleed this time, Mike Watt played with the same intensity and passion as he had fourteen years earlier and ended his set with the words, "start your own band." Jack was between music projects and Watt's words made him want to do just that. Later, a few blocks from the club, Jack passed a group of twenty-something guys and women climbing into their SUV across the street. The guys suggested naked hot tubbing and the women argued that it wasn't quite a naked hot tubbing night.

One of the women yelled, "Hey, is that you James?"

"Yeah," Jack yelled back, though he didn't know her, to see what would happen. "Are you going hot tubbing?"

"No," she said, giggling, then turned to the guys she was with and said, "James is one of my best friends." Jack waved to her as she got into the SUV and laughed at the absurdity of the moment.

"I wish I was James," he thought.

FOAM PARTY

Jack Waste's night began eons ago when forces conspired to create the environment necessary for his birth and survival on Earth so that he might one day read an ad in the newspaper about a Saturday night dance club "foam party" in Belltown and decide that this was what he wanted to do with his evening. He was curious from an anthropological perspective to see what the culture of such an event had to offer. He didn't expect much but was still curious.

Jack paid ten dollars to get into the club. A wave of humidity wafted up the stairs. It was *hot*, unpleasantly so, but he knew that a cold beer waited for him at the bar and descended confidently with the knowledge that if he collapsed, helpful strangers would intercede on his behalf.

Jack looked in at the foam party through the dance floor door. It was pretty crazy in there. People danced and disappeared in and out of a thick wall of foam that made it look like there was no boundary to the room and as if it stretched into foam infinity and darkness beyond. It was hard to see too far into the room because of the foam, making him wonder what was going on back there in the depths.

He ordered a beer and continued to stare through the door. A guy standing next to him said, "Dude, you HAVE to go in there," before disappearing into the foam with a drink in each hand.

Jack laughed and stepped over the barrier and into the foam. He was immediately struck with the fear of falling into strobe light-induced convulsions and suffocating a terrible death. The flashing lights were too much. The foam was too much. He couldn't see a thing except brief impressions of mounds of ceiling-high foam and faces caught frozen like photographs with each strobe flash.

He was no longer curious to venture further into the foam for a full immersive experience, so he turned and headed towards the exit and what he thought would be a quick return to the bar. There was a line of twenty people waiting to get out ahead of him, though. He looked at the small square of light that was the exit and tried to remain calm.

A twenty-something woman appeared out of the sea of foam and shouted to Jack over the din of pulsing music that she was getting claustrophobic. She appeared to be panicking. She leaned towards him and shouted, "Blow on my face, would you?!"

"Huh?" he shouted back.

"Blow this foam off my face, will you?!" she shouted again, more a command than a request, as if it was the only logical choice to help negate her claustrophobia. Jack blew some of the foam off her face and made a joke about dying in there. She said she could save his life because she was a nurse.

She grabbed his hand and pulled him towards the exit. To leave, you had to climb up five stairs set up as a barrier in front of the door to keep the foam from getting out. Once at the top of the stairs, a guy with a leaf blower blew the foam off your clothes and let you re-enter the club.

As they waited for their turn, she told Jack she had just moved to the area two weeks earlier, that some guys she met had invited her to the foam party, and that she hated it.

When she shouted "moved," Jack thought he heard the long "ooo" of a Minnesota accent, and shouted back, "so you're from Minnesota," to which she shouted, "how did you know that?," to which Jack shouted, "your accent," to which she shouted, "what accent?!" She climbed the stairs, had her foam blown off, and disappeared into the bar. It was Jack's turn. He climbed up, the guy pointed the leaf blower at him, foam went flying everywhere, and he was waved in. Jack looked down. There were bits of foam all over his clothes and shoes. He went to the rest room and looked in the mirror. There was foam in his hair and on his face.

"This is ugly," he thought, and laughed at the absurdity. After cleaning himself off, he returned to the bar. He asked the bartender if she enjoyed these foam parties. She said she thought they were cool when they first started but now she dreaded them because at the end of the night there was so much cleaning to do.

Jack sat on a stool next to the foam party exit. Two middle-aged women emerged. One lifted her shirt and flashed the crowd, which erupted in shouts of encouragement and applause from men and women both. A guy with a video camera asked her to do it again. She obliged, then joined her friends at the bar.

Jack watched as she drunkenly made out with the woman she was with, after which she grabbed a guy standing nearby in the crowd and made out with him, after which he turned and high-fived his friends. With her arms wrapped around the guy's waist, the woman then appeared to be surveying his friends for her next target.

Her friend sat on the stool next to Jack and told him that this was her bachelorette party and that she was getting married the next day. Jack didn't know what to say. The foam party was the last place in the world he imagined anyone wanting to spend the night before getting married.

Jack looked across the bar and saw the nurse dancing with a guy on a platform above the dance floor as Eminem rapped on the video screen behind her. The woman having the bachelorette party rested her hand on Jack's thigh while pumping her other hand in the air to the beat of the music. All around the bar, people were drunkenly making out. The word *herpes* went through Jack's mind. He felt relieved when the woman removed her hand and stumbled off into the crowd with her friend.

"Time to get out of here," Jack thought. He took one more glance into the foam party. He had no desire to go back into that madness. What had he been thinking? He felt lucky to have made it out alive. As his cab pulled away from the scene, Jack looked through the windows at all the people outside having the same dream, the same terrible wonderful foam party dream. He couldn't wait to climb into bed and go to sleep so he could wake and forget all he had seen.

GILLIGAN & THE PROFESSOR

Jack was walking across the Westlake Center park downtown one hot summer day when he saw a crowd gathered near a big white beach umbrella. People were lining up for something, so he walked over to see what was going on.

A table had been set up under the umbrella at which sat Gilligan and The Professor from the show *Gilligan's Island,* or rather, the actors who played them, Bob Denver and Russell Johnson.

People lined up to get their autographs. Miss Chiquita Banana sang from the balcony above wearing a hat made of bananas. It was all part of a promotion by the mall to celebrate summer.

Neither actor looked very happy, in fact, they were very obviously miserable. Gilligan wore his trademark sailor's cap and looked like a sad, wounded, caged animal. He didn't smile or speak to anyone who handed him something to sign.

The Professor signed copies of his book about the show, *Here On Gilligan's Isle,* also without smiling or speaking. People addressed them as "Gilligan" and "The Professor." Jack didn't hear one person call them by their real names.

One guy in the crowd leaned across the chain in front of the table and shouted, "Hey, Professor, did you know you're on channel 16?"

The Professor looked up from signing a copy of his book and said dryly, "Yeah, I think we've been in syndication for twenty years now."

Jack felt sorry for them and decided it was better to walk away than continue to participate in the sad spectacle by staring at them like everyone else.

The Professor looked pretty good.

Gilligan looked old.

LUCKY BEE

LUCKY BEE (THE AESTHETES)

Jack Waste wrote, "This immobility, this lack, this grand shortcoming, this settling for settling, for sleeping, for cozy nights at home. What has become of us? I could talk all night but then I would be like everyone else just talk talk talking and watch, watch, watching the movies and video games go by. We suspect we need a new grand adventure, but we don't seek it out except in entertainment.

Entertainment is the entrails of reality.

I could speak all night about why this is, but I would rather provide a perhaps not idyllic model of this problem at hand rather than trumpet myself as the hyperbole of solution. It is as simple as this: our imaginations have been stimulated beyond the point of any previously known stimulation. As a result, "reality" comes in a dull second place to the quad-aural worlds of our entertainment systems.

We should instead require action, proof, exploration, and adventure. No entertainment medium can have anything to say about anything anymore unless it is a live-time documentation of that activity. We require REALITY, and suffice it to say that the "reality" presented to us by television does not provide the modicum of hard facts that our own existence does. We are at the edge of known civilization. We are almost there, but there is nowhere further to go beyond what is known, and no spacecraft equipped to send us out to where we might really discover something.

Instead, we become entertainment aesthetes, lucky bees, lucky winners of products provided by others who also didn't have the chance to blast off out into the unknown, but who recognized early on their ability to create entertainment capsules for the rest of us to swallow. Culture vultures.

Did you see that film, did you hear that song, did you go to that show, did you download this, have you played that? The mind travels while the body stays behind.

So, what now? What next? Dive back into our imaginations? Dive back into our shells? Pretend we haven't seen the outer limits in films, books, and our own minds? Pretend the job makes sense, pretend the bus ride home at five with the nice meal and movie to look forward to while snuggling your cat or dog or boyfriend or girlfriend is enough? This is how we will live until we die? This is all we ask for? This is all we get?

Has science discovered without telling us that there *isn't* life elsewhere, that there is irrevocable proof that we are it? No. Are our leaders telling us *anything* we don't already know? Why should we continue to listen to what we have already heard so many times before? For this reason alone, they know nothing more than us.

So what then, what now, where to begin and what to do? Start a family? Pay back the student loans? Believe in rent, credit cards, pay per view, slot machines, a job well done, friends with equally-defined arts aesthetics who confirm our own ideas without acknowledging their veracity through actual experience?

Who is running the ship? Where is it going? This is not a test. Surely you will go home tonight and fall asleep, alone or with your snuggly snuggler, and you know what? I will be no different except that I will fall asleep later than you, I will stay up longer, and I will wake up whenever I want."

TO BE KNOWN OR UNKNOWN

Jack Waste preferred to be unknown. When did it become so popular to be known? Everyone in some way wants to be discovered but here, in this small town, what's the use? We already all know each other. The proper attitude to have if you decide to be popular is to guarantee a good time for all because it is a small town, because there is no anonymity, and because we all think we know all there is to know about one another, which prevents us from evolving further along than where we already are. And so the cycle goes on uncontained as we are boxed into small mental venues, catacombs in the honey maze, buzzing and pretending that we know the score.

Jack Waste wavered between creative chaos and domestic bliss. He craved the streets and bars and pool tables at night, and he craved the ecstasy of the dance floor when everyone had finally succumbed to the beat, but he also enjoyed epic nights at home when Seattle felt like a space port and he was just another traveler waiting for his ship take off or come in while listening to the rain and the sound of the other ships coming and going.

He was on track, off track, kiltered, offkiltered. All over town, couples were hunkered down, warm beneath their blankets and riding out the storm everyone else had either learned to take for granted or dreaded like cereal in warm milk. He kept walking and waiting, walking and waiting for the one he was walking and waiting to meet.

Again, he had made the usual mistakes. Just when he had started to slip into the uncomfortable anonymity and despair of someone who had no one to meet after work for dinner or drinks, he returned to thinking about the time before he felt bigger than the city and still overwhelmed by its formations of people moving around him in strange constellations. He only wanted to take his place in that mad charge of living a "regular" life. Years of transience and yearning had strengthened his mental fortitude, but when he arrived in Seattle he felt ready for a home base, a sense of belonging, and a voice who might speak his name at night as the world tilted at its insulting angles.

This is damnation and internal exile, he thought, mixed together into a thick paste that made it hard for him to breathe. What had become of the infinite city, the unknowable din? Why was he thirsty for waters he had known and lost? Why did the moon sometimes appear indifferent to his cause when he considered it to be his greatest ally? He tried to still his mind reading poetry by Gerard de Nerval, who kept a pet lobster at the end of a leash in Paris. Somewhere there was still mystery. They would meet and recognize each other, two jewels in the night meant to be bejeweled.

CHAPTER ONE

How could he explain the silence that hung over Seattle at night to someone who lived elsewhere? How could he explain the gray dreariness that got inside one's head for months at a time when the rainy season began until the city finally collectively revolted by throwing its energy into deep rainy season parties and pagan rituals? How could he explain the rhythms of the city to an outsider who was only there to confirm their outsider views by only seeing the obvious? Should he continue to live in a city that took so much explaining to make itself understood?

There were nights when he was in the flow of the city, walking with a friend after a night out. Broadway seemed to glow then with infinite possibility as faces both familiar and strange moved by in a slow motion choreographed dance. These nights were his favorites. Other times he felt like he was trapped in a painting of someone else's design and that all the faces were too familiar.

The sound of the rain would help things disappear until morning. He liked it when it rained and he was at home and at ease with the world and the silence that hung over everything, but he also craved sandy beaches, lazy afternoons in the sun, a hammock, cabana, and nowhere else to be.

He didn't trust the healthy optimistic lambs asleep in their beds unaware or choosing to ignore the dead man's axe at the end of the line. Everything was moving too slow, geared towards some unnatural rhythm and only the *promise* of an "average life span."

He turned on a documentary about jazz and was inspired by the looks in the eyes of the bebop madmen. He needed to hang out more often with other such mad people.

He loved and loathed the mundane damp of the rainy Seattle nights and their obvious effect on the rest of the population that created the illusion of a city bathed in sleep and lethargy with everyone tucked inside staring at their televisions on nights that might otherwise have been full of possibility.

When the rains arrived, everyone succumbed to the changes in weather and mood. Then, in late January or early February, people began to rise up against the laws of lethargy and slip earnestly into the costumes of their rainy season selves. This was the time of year when the rain didn't touch anyone, when everyone realized they were impervious to it, and when people left the house without thinking about using umbrellas. The nights from that point on were mirrors filled with reflections and neon light that bent, shifted, and gave way to a primordial soup of pagan pleasures. He was not there yet, though. It was still early January and on this particular day it was sunny outside.

The city had grown too small. Jack looked at the white Kubrick light that filled his windows, pictured all of Seattle in its lethargic glory, and knew that at some point he would walk out into the day and not be surprised by what he saw. The street kids would be begging change on Broadway, the students coming and going at the college, confident in their ability but completely unsure of the world, pretending, masking their illusions with illusions of illusions.

Did anyone really know what was going on? Was anyone really in control? Why had television and movies come to speak for reality? Why had people given up? Why did they spend 8.8 BILLION DOLLARS A YEAR ON MOVIE ENTERTAINMENT ALONE?

Jack's father had flown B-47 bombers in the Air Force. The B-47 carried nuclear bombs and the flight crews flew frequent exercises designed to prepare them to drop these bombs on their designated targets in Russia with the knowledge that they would then ditch their aircraft once it ran out of fuel and bail out to float down to a world gone nuclear mad.

Perhaps Jack had always sought such acutely melodramatic experiences in life. He did not find in the art world this same sense of realism. It was all "party pretend." Rarely did any of the "Dadaists" these days appreciate such extremes.

He loved the idea of the logistics of military campaigns, of having set targets and missions, of training for those missions and waiting for them to come up as contingencies in need of suitable responses. He was without an adequate mission and though his many probes and scout missions into the enemy's front lines had provided him with enough intelligence to confirm the fact that there was nothing there to make it worth invading their village, he still craved the spoils that every literary poet-warrior craved. Even a secret society needed its public victories once in a while.

He took great satisfaction in music, strangeness, and well-cooked meals, and if he was a true pilot-poet, he would thank those around him for the messages they sent over the past months and refer to them, in pilot/wing terms, as "attitude adjustment" that helped to right his experimental plane as it lifted off for the first time.

He would admit to being melodramatic, except the dramas felt real. During those long ago solitary Amherst summers, he became some kind of weird character in some weird book he had yet to write, fueled by delusion, Black and Tans, the flicker of lightning bugs in the humid night, and hopes of Surrealist love.

Why did he need so much proof now? Why did he want to both escape and recapture what he had left behind? Because he didn't want her name to be Whiskey.

The dead and dying were no wiser than the ones still alive, so where did that leave us, he wondered, none of us knowing a thing? Here was one possibility: onion rings.

JUST A DREAM

The sky was raining a beautiful rain, but the night was just a dream from which Jack Waste wished to fall into sleep. Earlier, Nick Cave had turned The Paramount into a cathedral and the world seemed alive and filled with possibility. The room stretched and bent and the songs were about the past, the present, the future, and infinity, and then it was over and he was outside walking in the rain. The world was filled with muted joy. He walked into Linda's, ordered a beer, sat down in the noisy middle of humanity, and let the waves of voices and music flow over him.

He had arrived at the sea of memory. The whole trajectory of his life appeared before his eyes. He had reached a strange summit after an oblique orbit. From here, he could see everything at once, his whole swath of experience. Despite all efforts both inept and concise to create a mode of consistency, those old friends Chaos and Ambiguity were still hanging around. Was he in outer space or waiting for liftoff? He didn't know. He finished his beer, returned to the night and walked home.

The city hardly felt like a city. All was hushed and quiet. Stillness dominated everything. He knew every night he left his apartment that he would step into that stillness and that it would envelope him with the same melancholy he wanted to escape. There was a certain pleasure in staying in.

From inside, the city appeared full of possibility and life. When he looked out the window he wondered if he was missing anything. Certainly nothing was missing him. He was hidden deep inside the city like a rock at the bottom of a cave. Water dripped a steady rhythm from the faucet into a bowl in the kitchen sink. It was all a dream.

DHDHDHDH

Where is the moment? Across the sea. We're in a submarine. It's all a dream, a movie of a dream of dreams. Exhilaration, free fall, it's a choreographed dance. Laughter is born out of the smoke of our fires. The stars watch from above as we sleep and welcome us into their circle when we dream.

Whatever we can imagine in our wildest imaginings is always outdone by the reality of the universe. We live in a time of change and barely recognize ourselves for the new selves coming our way. Life, noise, food, and sand; land is the sand that wants to lend a hand. A dolphin is a friend. Amen, amen. We come from liquid and return as sand, when we land, when we land, when we land.

The universe is made of revolutions and orbits. Galaxies revolve around each other. Moons orbit around worlds and worlds orbit around suns. Our lives revolve around each other's lives and projections of our realities and ideas. The universe, in turn, revolves around other universes. We can't begin to imagine what is out there, way out there, but forever is the place to go.

We need to escape the disease of influence and return to our original pre-influence thoughts. Perhaps there is no escape, but the dolphins and trees still seem free despite their connection to our self-destructive impulses. There are other words we are supposed to know, but we don't know how to shed the skin we're in.

Perhaps those words are elsewhere, on the outer planets of the hull of the universe where x-rays soothe and gather themselves before making the leap to pure mind, the semi-liquid state just beyond the hull where ambiguity is chaos twice divided by itself into something we have yet to imagine. The more we free ourselves from the disease of influence, the freer we will be to spend time in the fourth, fifth and other dimensions beyond.

Seen through the lens of the fourth dimension, the third dimension is illuminated by flecks of gold falling towards us from future millennia, yet we would rather devolve and hold onto the old ways rather than step through the beaded curtain's seeing eye. Lethargy and the bad habit of being human hold us back and make us act like tourists wherever we go instead of the super beings we could potentially be.

Rebellion does not come easy. What then, what next, what now? We are time travelers living and moving through the past, present, and future simultaneously. The frustration of not being able to go off world is overwhelming. Instinct pulls us towards the moon and the endless space beyond. We feel trapped in our earthbound garb.

The Earth itself is a starship hurtling through time and space. We forget in our thoughtlessness that the rock we are standing on is moving around the sun at 67,000 miles an hour. We strive so hard for understanding when the acceptance of worldwide mass bewilderment would suit us so much better. We allow external systems of thought to dictate our view of the world even when most of those systems are of small-minded and destructive varieties rather than the wide-eyed open states of minds our ancestors possessed before things had names and words to describe them...when states of mind still existed.

Perhaps we are exactly where we are supposed to be, moving at our own pace towards the future, some of us evolving into the star travelers we will one day become, some of us aware of our own stagnation as we watch others move ahead, and some of us, not aware of much of anything beyond the pulse of the pop culture current.

It is better to build than destroy, produce rather than consume, create rather than watch. Hypocrisy and lethargy hold us back. Unfortunately, they are as infinite as the stars.

PEOPLE MADE OF CLAY

It's better to start your day reading poetry so later you'll have something to say to the cashier at the bank who cashes your checks. In the meantime, keep scrubbing the dirt from your wall, it's no longer fall, it's no longer fall. You can do what you want in your own quiet way, you've just got to find a quiet cohort to count your money at the end of the night.

It was Saturday, time to pretend to get things done. Everyone was outside walking around. Jack Waste will walk today too, but it won't make the news. The world didn't know he was inside the inside part of his life and that he knew it was all made of clay and that one day we will wash away or be made into little clay people who walk around town blinking and nodding at the other little clay people walking around town blinking and nodding.

Today he wanted to go to the bakery to ask for a kiss. They used to give them out quite freely in the old days. He reminded everyone that these were the good old days, but no one seemed to believe him, which brings us to this: whose days *are* these? No one wanted to think, they just wanted to shop, stop thought, watch, and say about the other guy, HE'S fucked up, HE'S the one who's made of clay.

Well, nobody's real, and nothing is as it seems.

A BIT OF CALM IN THE SWIRL
OF AWKWARD TECHNICIANS

Jack Waste found solace in the supermarket. At the right time of day a calm superseded all as everyone wandered up and down the aisles searching for sustenance and things to make them feel cozy. It was the only time they were all truly choreographers, lingering here and there as they put together the perfect ensemble of tastes for their evening meals.

Most of the time you can look at the food in another person's cart, Jack thought, and know that you have nothing in common. Sometimes, though, you see someone who has pieced together a meal you wouldn't mind eating yourself and that you wouldn't mind sharing it with them.

Yesterday there was a supreme stillness at the supermarket. It felt as if they were all walking through a substance that was thicker than air but lighter than water. Nobody was in a hurry, there was nowhere to rush. The lines were long but everyone was patient. It was a change of pace and felt rather good.

The checkout clerk who usually had a bandage on the right side of his head where he was missing his right ear was no longer wearing the bandage. Jack ran his card through the machine and requested twenty dollars cash back. Even the clerk was feeling the calm. His eyes were wide and kind of glazed. He was lost in the moment too when he reached into his till and pulled out a hundred dollar bill instead of a twenty. The calm of the night was broken like a stone being thrown into a pond when he noticed his near mistake.

Once outside, Jack noticed that the world had returned to its normal crazy pace and when he turned around to look inside the supermarket he saw that everything had returned to its normal hustle and bustle as well. Why was everything moving so fast? All that misplaced energy was supposed to be spent on some grand undertaking, some epic journey into the furthest reaches of space, away from supermarkets towards other worlds where other beings weren't so connected to the everyday pace of time and where there were only endless days, endless nights, and lazy clocks.

SATURDAY

There's a madness in the air. Do you feel it?

THE OLD ARE DYING, THE DEAD KEEP GIVING THE END AWAY

Jack Waste wrote, "I want to escape the name of days and the tattoo of hours. I dream about the three sisters. After the time of false starts we were sent to the camps, where we were finally instructed in what it was all about. I have always been a thief wearing the concurrent garb of the technician at work at his controls. I have always sought to bring a sense of calm to the chaos, to open up the room by showing those who are inside it how high and far it actually extends. Every room is more infinite than we give it credit for. We hold ourselves back because we have been told not to expect much and even if we don't expect much what do we get in return? How many circles can we walk through before we realize it is a closed loop? The boundaries must be redrawn..."

Jack lay on his couch and stared at the window. He was unkempt. The day had swirled around him. Unexpectedly, he had come undone. The electric fan whirred as tiny raindrops lightly tapped the window. The streetlight outside looked like a giraffe with a necklace made of lanterns. Elsewhere, galaxies were in motion.

That morning, just before he woke up, Jack dreamed a long sequence of events involving a group of insane characters dressed in Technicolor suits. They were gallivanting about in a seemingly infinite white-tiled room that appeared to stretch for miles in all directions. Jack had a bag containing some pills, but when he reached in all the pills crumbled and he was left licking the powder that remained. He yelled at the group, "I am too infinite for this! I've transcended the mundane routine of everyday chores!"

Jack Waste wrote, "There is a strange light coming through the window. Its pinkish hue makes me feel like I am the only one alive inside a great closed eyelid. How long can this moment last? Everything is still. The light is dimming now. Night is coming. The moment is ending. Is it only the dreamers who know we are dreaming? Is it only the dreamers who know this is all a dream?"

WITHIN THIS MOMENT IS ALL MOMENTS

Jack Waste sat on a bench at Boren Park on 15th and wrote, "She was the empty porch swing. I had left my dark cave where I sat waiting for ideas, food, and desire. It was the end of a long period of mourning. One part of my life had ended and I had yet to become immersed in the next.

The phone did not ring. I wanted separation, lift-off, the falling away of stages as the Earth grew smaller behind me and I left everything behind and hurtled towards the far reaches of the universe.

I knew what to do with my time and solitude, I knew that I was waiting for the adventure to begin, I knew that I had to be awake at all times when I left the cave if I was going to recognize the moment when it began. I was both bored and fascinated. Who was I? I no longer knew. I was not any of the jobs I had. I was not my name. I knew there was something else beyond all this so-called "reality." I knew they would never talk about it on the evening news. I knew that all entertainment was designed to crush our urge to explore, to expand, to push towards the outer reaches, but I was without the proper ship. I was landlocked in between two sets of ideas: the mundane routine of illusions that everyone seemed intent on living to the fullest, and the edge I had discovered in the back of my mind where a hidden door opened up onto a plane of light and possibility.

I had found the room where life began. It was endless. There were no walls and no windows, and once I passed through the door into this room it was so vast that even the idea of the door and the idea of the room slipped away.

I found myself in the realm of pure sensation, far away from the land of ideas that needed words to exist. It is only a compromise on my part that I have decided to express these things in words now. It is done with the hope that some might follow and leave behind their own set of illusions in the pursuit of pure sensation, for it is only in sensation that we discover a limitless language that places no boundaries on our thoughts, ideas, and time.

I could not walk down the street without feeling as if I was going to go flying up into the sky. I no longer knew the meaning of the word calm. Everyone around me appeared to be having a good time. They appeared content and healthy. I assumed there was something wrong with me until one day I began to suspect that I had finally found my mind, not lost it. Those vibrations that ran through me made me feel as if the street was tilting beneath me. Day after day, I fought this feeling until I finally realized that I was at sea and that the sea was tossing me from side to side and making it difficult for me to sleep.

I could not sleep because I did not want to. I did not need to rest, I needed to be more awake, I needed to be on the lookout for the unknown shore, the shimmering eyes, the velvet caress. I was waiting for the wordless moment.

Language did not seem to facilitate much more than the everyday rote of routine. Yes please, thank you, no thank you, I would like one of these and one of those, check please... The bills that arrived in the mail said nothing about enlightenment. Everything was designed to keep us down, and then...there I was alone at sea, no longer dreaming of land, no longer dreaming of the unknown shore. I was simply waiting for it to arrive because I knew it existed. Why hadn't I learned a long time ago that the secret was to leave words behind?

I had found myself in a rough spot of endless waiting. I could see through my walls to the world that existed beyond but they were walls all the same. I did not think of my cave as a prison, I thought of it as a refuge. The world was the prison. My cave was escape.

People looked right through me and knew I had ceased to exist. I took this realization badly and retreated to the sanctity of my cave. It took a long time to realize that all the people who existed might have not existed in the first place, for who would have dreamed such a world of awfulness when all the powers of the universe rested on the palette waiting to be put into play? I closed the door and lay down in the dark to wait. I had to ask myself what I was going to do if the image I had in my head never came to pass in the outside world at large. What if I was deluded, what if there was nothing left but the memories that had led me to that moment in time? What if the dream I had of the world and what I expected from the world did not exist?

I had found friends long dead in the literature I read. I was looking for evidence of fragments of useful thought left behind by those who had come before. I was looking for true friends and found many. Would a recitation of their names help you in your own search? Perhaps, but you will have to roam your own aisles of your own libraries. I don't know who you are looking for, if anyone. Perhaps you are looking for me, and I am long gone as you read these words in the library or on your screen, letting my syllables dance in your mind as you try to imagine this moment, this dusk as the sun sets and I come to terms with this day and the fact that I cannot be where you are now.

Finding so many words from other times that spoke to me was both a blessing and a curse. A blessing because I realized I was not alone, that I had never been alone, and that I was surrounded in time and space by like-minded spirits; a blessing because there was now hope to continue my search for the rest of my fellow survivors from the wreck that stranded us here. I discovered these voices in poetry and stories, in the bending of words and language. I discovered that these voices, these unmet relatives, also believed in the evidence they had collected and understood they were communicating to spirits who had yet to arrive in the future. For a long time I thought it was sad that I could not know these people. I stared at their pictures and tried to hear the thoughts they were projecting.

I knew we were not lost because of the evidence I had found in libraries and books. These were maps designed by past travelers to lead us in the direction we are supposed to go. The future was that door I had always suspected, that moment in time where the angles of light and color fell into place when I noticed two eyes looking back from the other side of the door. It was disconcerting to find that she had arrived from the future and was looking for me and, at first, I continued on my way. I laughed out loud at the obviousness of our recognition when I got back to my cave.

And then, again, I was alone. I had found the door, stepped through to the other side, and turned around to return in the direction from which I had come. It was the past, again, pulling me back from the future, a stubborn tether holding down the balloon of eternity.

How can one be ready? The future does not arrive like an invited dinner guest. It simply appears. Suddenly the future is now and all you have to do is recognize it. I vowed to take note of these markers in time that came from the future unannounced. I had learned to recognize them but was still in the throes of digesting the code needed for their capture. If I could do this, I could transcend time and begin to see things happening before they happened. I was still a long way off, though. I had mistakenly assumed there was more to learn when she had arrived right in front of me. I recognized her but not the moment. Both our doors had opened from separate sides of different dimensions and we had peered through at one another without fully seeing what was on the other side.

But still, the future had arrived. I would not travel back in time to lament our childish misunderstanding of our dimensional ambassadorship. I simply reminded myself that I had been bestowed with this position and that it was now my task to learn how to operate on this plane.

What does one do when a story has begun, when its vibrations echo into shimmering configurations of light and shadow? The cement I stood on was no longer cement. It had been transformed into something pliant upon which my feet pressed lightly without fully sinking through.

Should I dive into it and try to retrace her steps or the portal from which she had arrived? Perhaps she was content with our initial encounter, perhaps it was all the evidence she had needed. Perhaps she was far ahead of me, perhaps she recognized the novice I was as I sat there near the stone lions contemplating my next move.

But then one of the stone lions moved, stretched and yawned, and I told myself to be content and return to my lair to wait, for the night was approaching and inside the dreams of in between days I would find the language that might be of use when we discovered each other next. I took off my shoes, lay my head down on the pillow and closed my eyes, safe in the knowledge that as I slept the message I required to see my way through would be delivered and that when I woke in the morning, the day I would float through would be the dawn of time and I would soon stand with her arms in mine on the warm white sands of the future.

OVERARC (THE LONG MARCH)

Time has no shape. We are ghosts floating through ghosts. On the street in front of Niketown, other ghosts pass me by. I'm always left thinking, "if I could fly, if I could fly, if I could fly."

Where is the simple room I always see in my mind? Books, table, chair, lamp, a simple room with a simple bed. I miss the you in you. You wanted to make a map. You wanted to make a map out of memories and beer. You used to be able to give directions. Now you point and say, "over there, memories and beer."

On the glacier, I had given up hope of being rescued. Shots here of a noose, cyanide pills, pistols, sunshine in the trees. I made a friend who offered to show me the way. Shots here of Heaven's Gate cult leader, the comet Halle Boppe, preparing to shed our containers, the purple shroud, liftoff, ascension. On the ship everyone was happy to see us. There was no confusion. When I woke up they were surrounding me, but still I could not see. They lifted me up and shined light into the dark corners. There was no turning back. Shots here of alien masks being removed.

Tabetha, Stacy, infinity, hyperspace. I returned to Earth and realized I'd been home all along. Belgium was now. I miss the Heather Graham days. So much was ruined, so much was lost. What was it all about? Mistakes. Learning. It was on! Belgium was now!

We are protected by the wall of memories. All that we have done, all that we have seen reminds us of who we are and who we are searching for. I'll send a messenger. I'll hold your coat when we're ready to leave.

Did we sleep forever and just wake up today? After millions of years in a suspended state, have we just now arrived? How many times can we keep waking up from this eternal slumber? Survivors of sleet and bone and hail, where is our peaceful garden? Mental land mines interrupt everything. I'm waiting for you in the lobby of my mind:

plush red velvet, brandy and wine. I think of you and finger my glass.

I try to remember the epic overarc of it all, even that last curve at the end of that dirt back road just before the soft serve ice cream stand on Route 9 right before the bridge over the Connecticut River between Amherst and Northampton.

Memories return to meet us, but there is also action, desire, angels to care for, angels to care for us, and strangers to mingle with or meet.

One afternoon at The Canterbury, two twenty-something couples sat at the booth next to mine. One couple was American, the other French. I listened to their conversation as I wrote and knew more about what they talked about than they did. I did not tell them this, though. It seemed important for them to think they were in charge of the world.

They talked about "films" as if they made them themselves and said things like, "I had a friend who worked in a video store in New York who told me..." and, "she won't watch anything with Vincent Gallo in it."

The French woman said, "I think Vincent Gallo is sweet." The American guy said, "That's your idea of sweet?" I sided with the French woman, I sided with Vincent Gallo, and a few weeks later, a woman I met and told this story to said, "you're much sweeter than Vincent Gallo," confirming what I already knew.

The French woman blew her cigarette smoke in my direction as Morrissey sang "How Soon Is Now?" from the jukebox. I thought about the rare dreary L.A. rainy night in 1985 when I first heard it on KROQ.

The bar felt like the last stop on the last bus line before the edge of the world. Beyond were only the cemetery, the view of distant mountains, and the bus coming back after it turned around. When it was time to leave, I turned left towards the life I was going to find in the opposite direction of the end of the line.

Another afternoon, I walked down Broadway past Hollywood Video to the corner of Broadway and John. A woman was talking to the security guard in front of the bank. When I walked by I heard her say, "It's not like I said to her it sucks to be you." While waiting to cross the street twenty feet and a minute later, a man and woman walked by and the woman said to the man, "It sucks to be you."

In 1999, the world cracked and sat on its edge. All its beauty seeped out like gold lava from an emerald egg. The new millennium was an echo despite its shimmering beginning. Wreckage is a beautiful word. She was my wreck. I was her wreckage and she walked away from me unscathed.

When I left the movie theatre after *Jesus' Son,* I saw the magic in all things. The film had reminded me. It had been a long time since I had seen a movie. I had wanted to be rejuvenated through images, and I was.

I walked down Broadway, taking it all in. Sitting on the back patio at Linda's amongst a crowd of strangers, New Order played on the jukebox. I was reminded of 1983 and the seventeen years since. 1983 sounded good but I was glad it was 2000.

People ate, drank, and talked. No one looked very worried or concerned. The world seemed quiet. I felt at peace and lost in its quiet mood. There were people I hadn't met yet who would one day be my friends.

Two days later, I woke on a friend's couch in Queen Anne after a night on the town. She sang two sad love songs at Sorry Charlie's. We made late night egg sandwiches on toast. I fell asleep with my shoes on. Life was good.

Noises from the train yard woke me: trestles, clanging. Strange pieces of strange dreams. I was nowhere, no one, liberated of context, apartment, belongings. Perhaps it was time to travel. Perhaps it was time travel.

Where are we going? We wait for the perfect mesh, the past that has yet to arrive. Is it in a bowling alley? The present embraces the past, but the future is where it's at.

The full moon watches over the present. I know I will not see you because the moon has made sure it will not be that kind of night.

Here I am in a moment that feels endless: wine and food in belly, she is reading a book, Sunday night, no reason to go anywhere, do anything else. The moment takes forever to pass instantly.

I caught glimpses, futures, worlds, universes within universes, futures within futures. The world's noise was my voice. I was alive inside the great nothing eye blink.

We are a parade of ghosts. Why do we hold on to so much we need to let go? Words are bricks and spit and bone. This moment, this feeling, this desire is real. What to exterminate: all non-literary romance, all non-collaborative creative activity, all forms of lethargic speech.

We are untethered, grounded, sane, insane, lawless, rulers, creators, destroyers, tranquil, chaotic, stupid, wise, peaceful, alive.

Arrays of word projectors need to be aligned towards the west of understanding. No more everyday experiences, bank statements, collection notices, past due bills. From here on out, just books and experience.

I have miles of untendered credit. Hope, heartbreak, and angst: 1987, 1990, 1999, 2003, 2007. Estimated value $2,000 an hour times 2,000 hours, a compromise estimate. Manuscripts (value unknown, but immaculate). A thousand miles of orgasm. We need forgiveness of all debt. Who will suffer when all would gain from a little bit more in our lives? Debt is an illusion but abundance is not. Abund us!

The candles disappear into the table. Drinking beer with Waltz comes to mind, eight years to infinity ago. Memory is a candle burning inside a donut. I miss timelessness, euphoria. I was once a great shoplifter.

In whose heart do we now exist, for we no longer exist in our own. Desecration of the cathedral of rules, the broken mirror of expectations, the salad of *I know nothing*, the entrée of *you know nothing too*, the dessert of *right on, it's all good*. It's almost happy hour, we'll be happy soon. Pure action, no nostalgia. Are you ready? Wanted: one getaway driver, dark hair and eyes.

I sat in Ileen's collaring a booth alone. Syracuse was playing basketball up on the TV and I was thinking of things to say, things to do, possible futures. A Mac and Jack later, I made my move for the door. Nobody noticed me leave, though they had noticed me alone and content in my both -- CONTENT! -- and therefore didn't fuck with me.

Syracuse won, going away in the end, the players finally listening to Coach Boeheim, and while I was dialing my voice mail number at the pay phone, a drunk guy smoking a cigarette looked at me and said, "Man, you're one ugly motherfucker!" to which I replied nonchalantly, "Yeah, but I'm full of love." His drunk eyes smiled as he laughed and high-fived me. I walked home immortal and alive.

Summation of the facts: the clock is too fast. I am neither victor nor neon bible salesman. I know what these words mean: holding hands, gifts left in the crook of a tree, Vegas!

Nectar, beer, salt and blood. I was alone, I couldn't escape, I felt a rhythm in the night. I was marching towards you. No longer a fugitive, it was an attack against lethargy, the long march, *Siege of the Castle of Love.*

I was a general (emperor?). Infinity had become routine. Strangeness, abandon, shores of the mind, banks of the river of thought. I went offworld on the first ship that offered us a ride. I was still holding on to old pastures, fields long gone, thoughts thought out. Life was not teriyaki in a box. Mountains called. River barges. Dissociation.

I jaywalked twice. A homeless kid looked at me and said: "Hallelujah!" The night was my room. I could do no wrong. The night was warm ocean water. I swam slowly, enjoying the ebb of the tide.

There were these hills. I saw them shimmer. I saw through them to the other side. It was a mirror. I was you and you were me. I wanted to climb but when I stepped I fell off. I didn't realize I was already at the top. I held your hand on the shore as we sang. The current was moving too fast. Why do we move so willingly into the future when it always turns into the past?

Love and death were no different in the first millennium. Life was slower then but the mountains were the same. Memories and the future simmer slowly. You can't rush soup. In the desert, life is boss. Is there really such a thing as a left and a right sock?

Tonight I can hear the music of the far off plains. The dark is filled with light. Tired of fighting, but there's no end to the fighting in sight. Will we be granted absolution, a time of grace? One day we will be heard.

Now we've come so far, and here we are. Contradictions abound. Everything is strange. No more acts of contrition. No more false hope. One day we will find the all-seeing eye, the all-knowing, unblinking eye.

A WALK DOWN BROADWAY

Jack Waste wanted to walk through the city all night but he had run out of city to walk. His perception of New York and San Francisco was that if he lived there he would be able to walk all night without stopping and without running out of city to walk.

In Seattle, though, one quickly ran out of walking room and had to come to terms with settling, with sitting down, with digging in. Some nights he felt like a jet running out of runway before takeoff.

He liked the rhythm of walking and the way it gave rhythm to his thoughts. He wished there was a way to download the novels he had written in his head while walking through all the cities of the world he had visited.

In Seattle, just when his thoughts began to get going, just when his blood was flowing and his heart was beating in rhythm with his footsteps on the sidewalk and the typewriter of the mind, it was time to turn around, time to come to terms with the evening and leave the page in his head blank.

The Space Needle was the city's mood meter. He had seen it pulsing and glowing with pleasure when the whole city was alive and partying and he had seen it look gray and pale when the city seemed to be asleep or in mourning or trying to wake itself up from its weather-induced stupor.

On this night, the sky was filled with sharp dagger rain clouds that moved like panthers beneath the peeking eye of the moon. These panther clouds knew it was not their time and that they should keep moving, as the moon would surely tell the sun about them in the morning.

Jack walked down Broadway. The world shimmered as everything moved in a choreography of jazz, motion, sound, voices exchanging stories, passengers in passing cars listening to music with their windows rolled down while the moon looked down and watched. Jack's legs felt solid against the sidewalk as he wove in and out of the other people moving down the street.

There was a long line at Dick's. Groups of people stood together eating their burgers and fries. He did not see one person who did not appear to be content. There was poetry in the night. Even the ones asking for spare change looked amused and even though something bad surely must have been happening to someone somewhere it did not feel like anything bad was happening on Broadway.

He crossed the corner of Broadway and John, walked past Steve's Broadway News where the browsers browsed and the clerk watched over the readers and the pulse of the street outside his door. He walked past Café Septieme, where almost all the tables were filled with people talking and where the waiters moved smoothly amongst them. He walked past the now sad and creepy Ileen's, which had closed its doors forever a month before. He paused for a moment to look in the window and thought of all the nights he'd spent inside taking in the universe as it wrapped its galaxy arms around all who entered with a welcoming embrace. He walked past a guy sitting in a doorway playing two flutes at the same time. In front of another store, a kid was playing a didgeridoo. Music cascaded out of the Broadway Grill. Books filled the windows of the Bailey Coy bookstore and browsers browsed its shelves.

For a moment, he pictured his own book sitting in the window on a Monday night as someone else passed by and looked in to see what was new. He wondered if he had enough for a book. Words and stories had been streaming out for years, but when would it be enough? He looked in at everyone eating sweets at Dilletante's and sipping margaritas at La Cocina. He had never been to Dilletante's and wondered if he would ever reach a point in his life where a cup of cocoa was the wildest part of his night.

Tonight he wanted to get some words down on the page. The nightlife would always be there waiting to welcome him back, and though he quickly ran out of Broadway and had to turn around and go back the way he came, he knew that on this particular night, this simple walk was just enough to get him into the rhythm of words. He continued down Broadway and turned left on John. Just past the locksmith's sidewalk mystery soda machine, he crossed the street and continued on up the hill.

The moon was content. It liked looking down on the world on nights like this when the "can you spare a cigarette" guy seemed to ask Jack Waste for a cigarette not because he didn't have any of his own or because he really needed one but because it just felt good to say the words.

BACKWARDS DREAM
(OUR LADY OF THE ASSASSINS)

She called it "this backwards dream," referred in passing to "her ghost," mentioned without explaining "her theory."

When Jack Waste asked, "Are you crazy?" she smiled calmly and said, "Yes."

He felt so far outside the moment that he was not sure it was real. He felt like he was above everything looking down until a door opened into her mirror.

When they interrupted each other and pieced together the fragments of their thoughts, they formed complete sentences. It felt familiar to be with her while it also felt strange.

There was a gray nothing to get lost in when autumn arrived: the discontinuity of mystery, the discontinuity of dialogue, the something of "has ended," the something of "has begun."

He did not see the chestnuts until they fell from the tree. He did not see the train until it left the station. He did not feel the shifting tide until the waves had overwhelmed him.

When she spoke he knew what she meant but asked for explanations anyway. What to say when things are so familiar they seem to arrive a minute before they do? What to say when words insult meaning and cease to serve their definitions?

He was a scrambling shell, a hollow horn. There was no "inside." All was illusion. The path was not really a path. The thought was not really a thought. The shell that hid the shell was not a shell.

If there wasn't drift or tow, there would only be "loose shavings." He forgot that he could say, "you've been on my mind" without having to leave mystery behind. He wanted to arrive at forest lake shores, holding hands, listening to the quiet waves while watching the falling leaves for scattered bits of her heart.

"Every landscape involves a story," she said. Making memories chase the sun, he walked past his fever of neglect. The future was arriving. Action.

Jack Waste chose the front entrance of the cathedral, not the back. He chose the heavy door, not the one on the left. She was sitting in the second to last row and turned to look.

What movie is this from? The cathedral scene, ah yes, the cathedral scene. Though he didn't stop to pray, please make a mental note, Lord, he chose the heavy door, and she was sitting there waiting for him.

We are far from horror though horror is all around. If we want to see it we mostly just walk among its memory and recollection in art. In the shrine candles burn, there is straw on the floor, the click of a telegraph at work, barbed wire on the walls, and we are lucky to be alive and dying.

Standing inside the replica horror train made him want to say he loved her. Fingers, clocks, and hands said "hurry" but she refused to rush and left him lapping, in luxury, yes, as all existence is beautiful, but he had already witnessed eternity, made friends with fireflies and worms and knew that this particular shore was meant to be seen with two pairs of eyes.

He waited to be guided even though they were guiding each other as they glided through days with no name that begged for a good night's rest.

Only in memory is the past easy. The future promises...what? We look for things to understand, rhymes, states of mind. How to explain that all his days had fallen away like rocket stages falling slow motion back to Earth? How to explain he was tired of margins, tired of time? How to explain the contradictions of terms?

He wanted to be near, to not speak. He was at war with time and the laws of the universe. Still, he hoped she'd been waiting to hear someone say, "red wine for two and a table with a good view."

PLEASE DO NOT PUT PEANUTS ON THESE STEPS (9/11/01)

As he walked home from the supermarket the night of the 9/11 attacks, Jack Waste saw a handwritten sign tacked to a telephone pole. It said, "There is more time than there is life."

When he reached the corner, there was another sign written in block letters on cardboard posted at the base of a set of stairs leading up to a house. The sign said, "Please do not put peanuts on the stairs." On the stair next to the sign was a small pile of peanuts. Jack turned and continued walking. He did not want to be mistaken for the peanut-leaver.

Jack pictured someone arriving at the bottom of the stairs with a bag of peanuts. Whoever it was read the sign, laughed, and scattered another handful before disappearing into the night, and in the morning, the people who lived in the house emerged to find peanuts on their steps.

They looked up and down the street, hoping to catch a glimpse of the culprit, then shook their heads and went back inside.

OCTOBER NIGHT

Jack Waste walked down Broadway and came face to face with the moon hanging low in the sky. Dark shadows danced over the bricks and waved hello as he passed. There was a pleasant calm vibe in the air but not many people were out and about. Since the attack on September 11, the streets were emptier at night than usual.

Near Café Septieme, a woman stood against a storefront asking for change. She looked like a puppet carved out of wood costumed in a black raincoat that came down to the top of her knees, stockings, and black orthopedic shoes. Her short gray hair was neatly arranged and parted to the side. On each lip was a smudge of blood red lipstick. She didn't seem real. Jack wondered for a moment if he was the only one who saw her.

When he dropped a few coins into her hand his fingers touched the skin of her palm briefly and ever so lightly. Her hand was cold even though she had just pulled it out of her pocket. Her eyes were empty and for the moment their eyes met during the exchange Jack felt an uncomfortable sensation pass through him. He continued down Broadway and made the big slow turn onto John, which always meant he was on his way home or on his way to the much more subtle diversions of 15th.

There weren't enough streets for Jack to wander, so he wandered the same paths again and again even though none of them were long enough to make him feel like he was arriving anywhere.

Still, he kept walking and kept his thoughts moving forward, as they both went hand in hand. If he could only get the words down on paper that ran so smoothly through his mind when he was walking, he thought he might finally get somewhere.

Jack passed the Mystery Flavor soda machine in front of the locksmith shop, but didn't stop to put in any coins. It was almost always strawberry and he didn't expect tonight to be any different despite the chance that it might be another flavor.

The moon hung over John, perfectly centered, a bright white eye staring down, just the least bit tired, its lid sagging as the world waited for it to fall asleep.

Jack walked through the shadows of back streets lit only dimly now and then by a jack-o-lantern on a house's porch. It felt like there were ghosts in the air.

Not far from his apartment, he started a bit when he heard a noise from the alley. He flinched and turned to look, having the sensation that someone was emerging from behind, but there was nothing there but a shopping cart someone had pushed home from the store and no sign of anything that might have caused the noise. Still, since he was close to home, he walked a little faster and looked forward to his dark windows being filled with light.

It was the first real October night.

THE RELUCTANT MONK

ADVICE TO AN IMAGINARY DAUGHTER

Don't be crazy like me. Don't be crazy like your mother. Take your madness out on the world. The spur of the moment will bite deeply into you. Don't retreat from its spell. It only wants to lead you towards experience.

Your mother raised rabbits underneath her bed. Do you remember them nibbling at your toes and doing flips and dances as you crawled on the floor and played amongst them? Do you remember the sound of your mother's wind chimes making you smile when she put you to bed? Your mother was a happy cloud of gentle kisses. Do you remember?

I remember one day when I felt like I was going to fall into the void. It was a momentary state of weariness, but it seemed to take a long time to pass. We sway over moments like wind over a precipice and try to keep from falling in. I was three minutes, sometimes three seconds, behind the moment, and I missed some of those chances to break free from malaise into experience.

Not that I was without memorable experiences, just the opposite, but sometimes I failed to live in the moment, sometimes I was slow to wake. Come midnight, when most of my friends were already asleep, I was left to wander alone in the company of the other late night wanderers and seekers. There was certainly beauty in those moments.

Sometimes I wandered aimlessly through the day, other times with purpose, even if it was sometimes an aimless purpose to just wander aimlessly. Days and days of moments, nights and nights and hours and minutes and seconds, every one filled with something going on, things to watch, things to experience, memories to collect and reflect.

Anthems, love songs, and jazz solos played on the radio. I fell asleep and woke up to a new day. I had felt for a long time that nothing I wanted to happen was happening. I didn't realize that I was preparing for those things to happen. One day I began to experience moments of precognition, signs that I was finally arriving where I was supposed to be.

Things I had dreamed about began coming true. I was prepared, done my homework, and waited long enough. Isn't it strange that you once didn't exist, and yet the whole universe was just waiting for you to arrive?

And now here you are.

It's all for you.

THE RELUCTANT MONK

Jack Waste was becoming a reluctant monk. He felt like he was stuck in some kind of nowhere zone between an old and new reality.

It was all so simple, it seemed, but it was also very hard and he often felt like he was out of the loop. He was tired of feeling like a free radical, floating endlessly from possibility to possibility, never fully acting on the possibilities that appeared and urged him to live life fully.

He sometimes felt like he was floating through the universe, the only survivor of his home world, hoping to find a new home planet. The days were running away with the nights. He wanted to catch up and make them his.

Jack couldn't remember where the day began, what he had done with it, or if time even existed. No, that wasn't it at all, or it was only a part of it. He sat at his desk and wrote and tried to figure things out. He felt a spiraling inward, a gross dissatisfaction, as if there was an idea or realization of something struggling to set itself free.

He wrote and wrote but none of the words felt right. The television sat against the wall, urging him to turn it on, but Jack wanted to write. He sensed all the images that were flashing across the screens of the world at that moment. So many images!

"As you read this," he wrote, "what is happening outside your window, next door, across the street, in another city, on the far side of the Earth, on the dark side of the moon, on other planets, in other universes, in civilizations beyond the edge of what we know exists, beyond the edge of the forever that is beyond the furthest forever that we can ever begin to imagine, beyond that, and even nearby, in other dimensions?"

Jack capped his pen and imagined he was falling backwards. He imagined himself flying low above the ground, above canyons, rivers, trees, and mountains. The sun was behind him, setting red against the horizon.

A mesa appeared in the distance. Standing on top was a lone figure, her arms at her side, head bowed. She looked up as he flew through her as if she was mist or smoke. His soul now contained her soul, and vice versa.

He felt alive and new. She joined him and they flew, together, up.

A DAY ON EARTH

Jack Waste knew he had to write something. He sat down at his desk and thought about his day. The world was inhospitable and the humidity made him feel slow.

All day, people appeared to be lifeless, simply moving through space and time with no clearly defined motive or purpose, and everyone looked visibly affected by the heat.

He had sent some of his poems to several literary journals in various parts of the country. He wondered if any of them would find a home.

The saxophone on the radio reached into his head and pulled his thoughts to a beach at dusk with an orange sunset. Portuguese fishermen grilled sardines, drank beer, and made sardine sandwiches on baguettes.

Old Mercedes Benz taxicabs waited to whisk him away from the beach. The Rock Of Gibraltar shimmered in the near distance.

He wanted to go back in time to the music store and buy that sweet bass amp he didn't have enough money for at the time. He wanted to go back in time to the second hand store and buy that big velvet painting of two flying black dogs with white wings.

"A light breeze out of the southeast," the man on the radio said. "The pressure is falling." Words fought each other on the page; feuding words, parrots on popsicle sticks. It was late. Jack turned off the radio and went to sleep.

Outside, a light breeze out of the southeast passed over the city and the pressure continued to drop.

WHAT USE?

"What use writing it down," Jack thought, futility creeping into his head. "Just keep writing," he told himself. That was the answer. His notebook sat waiting on the desk. "Nothing matters. Everything matters. I know nothing. I know everything. The world is filled with contradictions." He lay down on his bed and stared at the ceiling. Things would come together. Time would take care of everything. He just had to keep writing. Bit by bit things would become clear. "A novel is an absurd obsession, a jaunt into madness. While you are writing, you miss things happening in the world. When you are out in the world, you miss things happening in the novel. It's a world of contradictions."

EVIDENCE OF DECAY

Jack picked up his pen and wrote, "Leaves fell from the trees when they turned brown. Crickets chirped until December, but in December there was only one cricket left. Children with cap guns fought long skirmishes up and down the street. Sunlight walked through windows and rested on wood floors just long enough to fall asleep and be taken away by the night.

Sometimes the moon was a sliver. Sometimes it was an eye. Cats wandered through back alleys and slept on the hoods of parked cars. Some houses were dark, some were filled with light, and someone somewhere lit a cigarette and sat back in their chair to inhale."

INTO THE FRAY

Jack Waste woke up the next morning and wrote in his journal, "Why must the novel be a neatly-packed bundle of twigs? Life is sloppy, a tatter-worn fray with no clean edges and no real conclusions—The Big Everything. It's ridiculous to think that one must wear two matching socks. The writer who lives a frayed life should be allowed to write a frayed book. A novel can be like a painting, a sound, a can opener, or a wound. It can make sense or it can make no sense. A book can be wicker, rust, or jazz; trumpet, grass, or steel; tarnish, potato mash, or scotch. Its flesh, lunch to some, a snack of ideas to others, can be a shock or glint of recognition, verification or negation of one's ideas, strewn litter or a napkin holder, a little nothing or a bit of honey to take the bite out of a sour dough day."

A TOKEN OF OUR APPRECIATION

The novel may be timeless or it may attempt to possess past, present, and future all at once. Readers should feel free to edit, rewrite, change the order of chapters and sentences, burn or rip out pages they don't like, or read favorite passages aloud naked at the top of their lungs through a megaphone.

Readers should feel free to copy the book and pass it along to friends and strangers as a token of appreciation. It is hoped that at least seven times in one's life, one will approach a stranger on the street and hand him or her a copy of one's favorite book wrapped in nylon or newspaper, foil or fur, lace or satin, sock or plastic wrap.

This is the least that can be done.

THE TROUBLES (W.T.O. RIOT DIARY)

132

THE TROUBLES (W.T.O. RIOT DIARY)

"Like most of us, I was a seeker, a mover, a malcontent, and at times a stupid hell-raiser. I was never idle long enough to do much thinking, but I felt somehow that my instincts were right. I shared a vagrant optimism that some of us were making real progress, that we had taken an honest road, and that the best of us would inevitably make it over the top."

"At the same time, I shared a dark suspicion that the life we were leading was a lost cause, that we were all actors, kidding ourselves along on a senseless odyssey. It was the tension between these two poles--a restless idealism on one hand and a sense of impending doom on the other--that kept me going."

--Hunter S. Thompson, *The Rum Diary*

NOVEMBER 27, 1999 (SATURDAY)

Jack Waste stood on the putting range at the Palm Springs Airport, waiting to board his flight to Seattle. He made several long twenty foot putts. A well-tanned older gentleman in golf clothes walked by, gave Jack the thumbs up and said, "Nice putt."

After some delay, the boarding call for his flight was announced and he walked out onto the tarmac towards the plane. There was something exhilarating about walking out onto an airport tarmac. He loved the feeling that the wide vista of space stretching towards the horizon inspired as well as the fact that he was being allowed to go somewhere and see something he normally wasn't. Every day of the week to come would have a similar sensation.

They were running late and he began to wonder how much of Stereolab's set at The Showbox he was going to miss. As they began their final approach, he looked down and saw the city below. They disappeared into the clouds for a few minutes as they looped around and flew towards the airport. Jack looked down and saw that they were above Capitol Hill where, from his apartment, he sometimes looked up to watch planes coming in as they made their final approaches. He pictured himself down there on Broadway, walking around, living his life. It was all so small.

He finished reading Hunter S. Thompson's novel *The Rum Diary* on the bus from the airport and, after arriving downtown, checked his bag at the coat check. Stereolab was well into their set and playing "Blue Milk" when he walked in. Jack's friends said it had been a wild show so far, but he wasn't feeling it. He had travel adrenaline rushing through his veins and was still processing the fact that he had just been up in the clouds a half hour earlier.

"People seem kind of out of it," Jack said to his friend Ian when he ran into him at the bar, "I thought there would be a feeling of chaos in the air when I got back."

"Tonight is just the calm before the storm," Ian said. "Wait until Tuesday."

It felt like a good time to cut his losses and go home early. Jack picked up his bag from the coat check and hailed a cab in front of the club.

It was the best cab ride Jack ever had in Seattle. The driver played loud Cuban music and drove fast as he zigzagged in and out of traffic, seemingly intent on getting him to his destination as quickly as possible.

After he dropped him off, Jack stood in front of his building for a moment to get a bit of fresh air and look at the Space Needle. The neighborhood was quiet.

NOVEMBER 28, 1999 (SUNDAY)

Jack woke up feeling tired and empty. Something was missing for him in Seattle. Perhaps he was missing from it. It didn't help that he still had feelings for his ex-girlfriend, nor that she had started to see someone new, nor that she lived two floors directly above him in the same apartment building. Jack did his best, but that was hard to deal with. On top of that, his birthday was coming up, the first he would celebrate alone in five years. He felt emotionally ragged.

He went through his pockets and threw out the detritus he had gathered, which included gum wrappers, receipts, and his boarding pass, on the back of which was written, "NOTICE: Please retain this stub and your ticket receipt as evidence of your journey." Evidence of your journey. Jack liked that.

He walked down Broadway and felt like he was new in town and didn't know anybody. He was lonely and depressed. A W.T.O. protest march moved slowly but noisily down Broadway. Jack walked on the sidewalk along with them, read their signs, and looked at the faces of the demonstrators. It didn't feel like a protest as much as a celebration.

After a few minutes, he got tired of watching the marchers and decided to go to La Cocina to nurse his travel hangover with a burrito and refill after refill of Diet Coke.

As he read the Sunday *Seattle Times* articles about what those of who lived in the city could expect in the way of demonstrations during the coming week, he remembered that he had been invited by his friend Curtis to be one of eleven Santa Clauses participating in the big protest march on Tuesday. Curtis's idea was to assemble a group of Ambassadors of Good Will from the North Pole to participate in the march.

After lunch, Jack stopped at a pay phone and left a message on Curtis's voicemail. "This is Santa Claus reporting for duty," he said. When he returned home, there was a message from Curtis telling Jack there would be a meeting at his place at 7:30 the following evening.

Jack turned on the news and watched as the newscasters discussed how the W.T.O. conference might affect traffic around the city. An interview with Mayor Paul Schell followed in which he said he was optimistic that it would be a peaceful event that would show the world an image of Seattle at its best.

NOVEMBER 29, 1999 (MONDAY)

Jack ate dinner at Taco Time, two soft chicken tacos and an order of tater tots, and walked up to Curtis's for the meeting. He did not consider himself to be very politically active except around election time, and though he had learned about the related issues leading up to the week, he was more intrigued by the Dada and Theatre of the Absurd qualities of Curtis's concept and seeing what was going to happen than making a political statement like the more serious demonstrations against the W.T.O.

When he entered The Vodvil Theater where Curtis lived, Katie was writing the evening's agenda in magic marker on a big piece of paper taped to the wall: Group Safety, Media Messages, Tactical Strategy. Jack hadn't expected a meeting with an agenda. He thought he was just going to pick up his Santa outfit, find out where they were going to meet, and throw themselves into the fray the next morning, but there were eleven people present and everyone had different ideas about what being an Ambassador of Goodwill from The North Pole meant to them as it related to demonstrations against the W.T.O.

They cracked open bottles of beer and discussed various opinions for what they wanted to do the next day, which of the several different marches they wanted to take part in, and what to do if there was "trouble." In the end, the group decided to meet at seven in the morning at The Lux coffee shop in Belltown. They would then walk down to the Pike Place Market and join one of the marches that were going to start there.

The high point of the meeting came after Curtis suggested they try on their Santa outfits. They got into their costumes and quickly fell into character, ho-ho ho-ing and laughing all the way. Jack set up his camera for a few group shots, raised his fist into the air as the camera flash went off, and The Santa Eleven were born.

Jack's brother gave him a ride home and said he would pick him up at 6:45 the next morning. Jack looked up at his ex-girlfriend's window for a moment and wondered what she was up to. He wanted to open the apartment door and find her at home with things the way they were when they lived together, but she was up there with the new guy. Jack sighed and went into his apartment. He wasn't feeling too excited about having to wake up so early. Why didn't they just agree to meet a little later in the morning? Why had he agreed to do this in the first place? He looked at his Santa suit, shook his head, and laughed. What had he gotten himself into?

He climbed into bed, set the alarm, and turned off the light. It was raining outside, the kind of rain that made it feel good to be warm inside and in bed. He fell asleep listening to the raindrops as they tapped hypnotically on the ground outside the window.

It was a very peaceful sound, and though he was sad and alone, he finally felt happy to be back in Seattle.

NOVEMBER 30, 1999 (TUESDAY)

The alarm went off at 6:15. Jack hit the snooze button a couple times, fell back asleep, and finally, when it was time to get up, lay there and listened to the rain while cursing himself for agreeing to participate in the Santa Claus activity. He pondered resetting the alarm for nine o'clock and walking downtown later by himself. He didn't think it would be too hard to find ten other Santas walking around the streets.

He turned on the news and looked at live footage of crowds of people gathering at different points across town to join the protests. He realized then that it was happening, it was for real, and began to feel excited enough to wake himself up and start getting ready. He didn't know what to expect but was excited for whatever was going to happen. He took a shower, got dressed, and put on his Santa Claus costume over his clothes.

He heard his brother's car idling outside and pulled the shades back to see three Santa Clauses peering back at him. They all laughed when they saw Jack in his outfit and beard looking back at them. He grabbed his accordion and umbrella, locked the door behind him, and adjusted his beard as he walked to the car. Katie, Curtis, Joel, Eve, and Jack all laughed as they pulled away from the building.

They drove downtown in the rain, parked near COCA, and walked to The Lux coffee shop. When they arrived, there were seven other Santas drinking coffee and adjusting their costumes in front of a mirror. The baristas all had amused smiles on their faces.

The group assembled for a few minutes of "Santa Calisthenics" and jokingly stretched the arms they would use to wave to the crowd, then practiced holding their bellies and ho-ho-ing.

A few minutes after seven o'clock, they headed down 2nd Ave. towards the Pike Place Market and waved at the drivers of passing cars as they walked.

Curtis carried a huge sign he had painted. On one side was the word BUY; on the other, he had painted BYE over the blue sphere of the Earth. Some people honked and waved from their cars as they passed. Others looked with confused expressions on their faces.

When they got to the Pike Place Market where the march was going to begin, they found that everyone had already left. They continued on their way and eventually caught up with the rear of the pack. When people saw eleven Santa Clauses approaching, smiles appeared on their faces.

There was a mix of fear, rebellion, and excitement in the air. They were walking down streets and sidewalks normally occupied by drivers and pedestrians going about their morning business. Chants and cheers filled the air. People clapped and played drums. It was a circus.

Jack was a very tired and grouchy Santa Claus. The others seemed to be more fully in character, holding their bellies and laughing loudly as they moved through the crowd. Jack's emotions were tempered by the weight of the break-up even in the midst of this circus of thousands and he felt as if he was watching everything from a distance.

When he did tune more into what was happening, he got the feeling that no one in the streets knew where they were going or what they were doing. There was no shape to the day yet and it felt like everyone was just coming to grips with how many people had showed up and that they were now waiting for something to happen. It felt like they were walking towards an unknown fate. It was an exhilarating but disconcerting sensation.

Jack was amazed by how many people in the crowd he either knew or recognized from around town. It appeared that everyone connected to his immediate and extended social circles had taken the day off to be there.

When they reached the corner of 5th and Pine, Jack saw Ian leaning against the Old Navy store, watching the crowd. He smirked approvingly and gave them a nod as they passed.

It felt good to be walking down the middle of the downtown streets, but Jack felt tired, grumpy, foolish, and giddy all at the same time in his Santa Claus outfit.

It dawned on him that if they found themselves in the middle of any chaos that it might not be such a good idea to be wearing a costume. Maybe it would be better to blend in with the crowd.

Hundreds of people raised their cameras to photograph them as they passed, though, so they seemed to be doing a good job of drawing attention to their group.

As they walked by the apartment building on the corner across from the Paramount Theatre, Jack saw that riot police had formed a wall in front of the building's entranceway. They held long wooden clubs, were wearing black ponchos, gas masks, and helmets, and appeared faceless and imposing.

The Santas walked down to the Westlake Center Christmas tree and paused to take a group picture in front of it. After posing for several people who also wanted pictures taken with them in front of the tree, they noticed small groups of people in suits holding briefcases and mingling together across the street. W.T.O. credentials hung from their necks. They were delegates trying to get to their meetings, unsure how to proceed.

Some protestors confronted them, yelling and pointing accusingly, "Delegates!"

They walked up 5th Ave. to 5th and Pike, where a line of standing riot police were facing off against a line of protestors sitting with their arms locked on the ground in the middle of the intersection.

The Santas stood behind the protestors and formed a line of their own. Jack saw one of the riot police smile behind his visor after he saw them.

A limousine tried to pass through the crowd but another line of protestors formed to keep it from getting through, and leaned against it, yelling into the windows and pounding on the hood. A police car moved slowly through the crowd fifty feet ahead. Suddenly they heard the sound of one of its windows being smashed. Jack saw the blur of someone dressed in black running away from the car. Some of the crowd scattered. Others ran towards the police car and surrounded it.

Katie yelled, "Santas!" the signal to gather together and decide what they wanted to do next. They had all agreed that they wanted to stay away from any trouble, but now that it was happening right in front of him, Jack was drawn towards it to see what was going to happen next.

Less than thirty seconds passed following the smashing of the police car's window before a police S.U.V. with tinted windows sped into the intersection and screeched to a halt. Its doors opened and ten riot police with laser-equipped M-16's got out and ran towards the police car to defend its occupants. They ran right past Jack's group, oblivious to the eleven Santa Clauses, and surrounded the car looking serious and determined.

Jack's heart pounded and he felt compelled to follow the action and see what was going to happen, but the other Santas wanted to move up the street. It was a smart decision.

He was surprised by how drawn to the danger he felt now that they were in the middle of it when just an hour or so earlier he was wishing he could stay in bed.

Nicholas ran into the fray with his camera to take a picture. When he returned, they moved up Pike towards the Sheraton Hotel and gathered near the big bronze teddy bear in front of F.A.O. Schwartz. Riot police guarded the entrance to the hotel where Jack was once a banquet waiter. He saw the head of the banquet department standing on the corner staring at the scenes unfolding in front of his hotel.

By this time, somewhere around 9:30 a.m., there was a palpable feeling of impending chaos in the air. Nerves were on edge. The day had shifted to a different level. Jack looked quickly from face to face and corner to corner as he tried to anticipate who would start the trouble and where it would come from. Would a bomb go off? Had anyone in the crowd brought a gun? There was no center to anything, and no script. The day was beginning to find its rhythm. Order was breaking down even as the illusion of order remained in the guise of the faceless riot police at their stations. It felt like the day had dropped acid and that its effects were just beginning to kick in.

A group of people wearing black clothes and masks stashed bags of something in a garbage can near the teddy bear and spray-painted the words First Aid on the side. The Santas didn't know if they were planting a bomb or if they were about to instigate some kind of action that might get them caught up in something they didn't want to be caught up in, but the bags turned out to be filled with bottles of water mixed with baking soda to pour into peoples' eyes if tear gas was used. Another group of five black-clad people stood on the corner wearing their own gas masks. The words First Aid were painted in red letters on their sleeves. They were waiting to help those who might be struck down.

A group of W.T.O. delegates ran through the crowd with terrified looks on their faces after being spit on by a group of protestors. Another group of protestors converged on the scene shouting, "No Violence!" and, "Do Not Spit On The Delegates!" The delegates gathered at the corner where a group of uniformed police officers formed a circle and escorted them away to safety.

The lines were being tested as some in the crowd instigated confrontations. The "rules" were being thrown out the window. Anything could happen now, Jack thought. The scene was simultaneously horrifying and beautiful, like a Bosch painting. Jack wanted to see chaos unfold. From where did this feeling spring? What primal need would the desire for chaos fulfill? He felt disappointed when it was time to leave the downtown area and walk to the 5 Spot on Denny, where they were to meet a late-arriving Santa and go to the labor rally at Memorial Stadium in the Seattle Center. It felt like they were leaving a concert after the opening act and before the main show began, though Jack had no idea what they were going to miss.

They walked down 3rd Ave. towards the Space Needle. Downtown was void of its usual activity. All the stores they passed were closed. There were very few cars and pedestrians. The city felt a little bit like the Los Angeles of *The Omega Man* with Charlton Heston, in which he plays one of the only survivors of a biological disaster. As they passed a construction site, a worker looked through a chain link fence and said, "I want a Lear jet and a helicopter."

It was now 10:15. The Santas walked into the 5 Spot and were welcomed by the early morning drinkers and diners with applause and laughter. The bar was filled with union members waiting for the labor rally to kick into gear. The beat of James Brown's "Sex Machine" filled the room.

They sat down at a couple of booths, ordered schooners of beer, and watched the television as police used tear gas on the protestors near the Sheraton Hotel where they had been standing just fifteen minutes earlier. They shot rubber bullets into the crowd and hosed people down with pepper spray. Tear gas filled the air.

It felt good to be sitting in a bar at 10:30 in the morning dressed as Santa Claus drinking beer with ten other Santa Clauses while the city erupted into chaos. James Brown screamed and people bobbed their heads and swayed their hips, including a couple of the Santas. It felt like the beginning of a crazy party and just as he had wished they weren't going to leave downtown, Jack now wished they weren't going to leave the bar.

There were two closed circuit televisions bolted into the wall of the bar connected to cameras inside the adjoining laundromat. They watched the monitors and laughed with the rest of the people sitting at the bar as their friend Jim changed into his Santa Claus outfit. It was time to go. They gathered together outside the bar and greeted him with a round of ho-ho-ho-ing.

People in the crowd continued to approach the Santas for pictures as they walked beneath the monorail and past the Experience Music Project construction site towards Memorial Stadium. The plan was to listen to the speakers in the stadium for a while and then follow the Anti-Fascist Marching Band when the labor union march headed back downtown.

After spending some time in the stadium, which was as packed as any headlining act Bumbershoot Festival concert Jack had been to, they found the band warming up inside the Seattle Center House, which was abuzz with activity.

People of all ages and walks of life were gathering to join the march. Jack saw school kids ditching school, workers ditching work, artists, musicians, and a small contingency of topless women who were protesting some aspect of the W.T.O.'s agenda.

They waited in the crowd with the band for a long time as the marchers filed slowly out onto the parade route. Jack played his little accordion with gusto along with the band. The mood was festive and tribal. Soon they were moving down 4th Ave. towards downtown and saw themselves on live television filmed by the Channel 5 cameraman as they passed by the news truck and looked inside at its live feed monitor.

A few blocks later, they agreed that a bit of rest sounded like a good idea, so they broke off from the march and walked into the Two Bells Tavern. It was now 1:30. Like the 5 Spot, it was filled with labor union members also taking a break. They ordered a couple pitchers of beer and plates of french fries and sat down to watch the parade of humanity walk by outside.

Some of the Santas made phone calls on the bar's payphone while others stared into space and nursed their beers. Nicholas sat at a booth filled with union members and talked to them about the march. A half hour later, they rejoined the march, which hadn't yet finished spilling out of the Seattle Center grounds, and headed back towards downtown. The mood had changed considerably since they were there earlier. There was less of a police presence and it felt like the marchers were in control of the streets.

The Anti-Fascist Marching Band played as they walked up Pine. Skerik and another saxophonist fell into a primitive trance vibe backed by the drummers' convulsion-inducing assault while everyone moved in unison towards the Paramount Theatre, where the Santas gathered near the entrance and sat on the curb. Photographers and videographers gathered around like paparazzi and pointed their cameras at them.

Someone shouted that the police were using tear gas a few blocks away. Jack caught a whiff of it as it wafted up the street in the wind. It wasn't such a bad sensation and had an almost pleasant, alluring taste and odor. People walking up from downtown, though, covered their mouths and coughed, their eyes red, swollen, and filled with tears.

The scent of tear gas at that moment felt like it was part of the festive atmosphere the way the smell of popcorn and cotton candy fill the air at a carnival. They did not know what was going on in front of the television cameras a few blocks away, where things had descended into a state of total chaos as some of the non-peaceful demonstrators broke windows, turned over dumpsters, started fires, and spray painted storefronts with the Anarchy symbol.

They did not know that the police were shooting rubber bullets at point blank range into the crowds of protestors, nor that mass amounts of tear gas and fountains of pepper spray were being expended in an effort to clear the crowd from the streets. By this time it was close to 4:30 in the afternoon. The sun was beginning to set and people were streaming up from downtown. Most of the Santa Eleven called it a day. Only Katie, Curtis, and Jack remained. There was word going around that the police were tear-gassing people at 6th and Pike. Jack wanted to walk to the corner of 6th and Pine and look down the street to see what was going on. The air was thick with the scent of tear gas now.

DJ Jason Justice rode by on his bike, just off work. Jack chatted with him for a bit and then he rode off intent on checking out the action up close.

Jack stood with Katie and Curtis on the corner next to Barnes & Noble and watched as panic spread through the crowd and caused it to flee suddenly towards them like a herd of gazelles being scattered by attacking lions.

It happened fast but it was clear that there was nothing to do but turn and run. They started to bolt across the street but a self-preserving instinct kicked in and Jack grabbed Katie's sleeve, pulled her towards the building, and yelled to Curtis to join them there so they didn't get trampled. They pressed themselves against the side of the building as the crowd streamed by. As quickly as the crowd had bolted, it came to a stop. Jack had never witnessed such mass panic in person before; it was frightening. Some storefront windows were smashed and people were yelling. They smelled more tear gas in the air and decided to move up the hill away from downtown with all the rest of the people who appeared to be calling it a day. It didn't feel different from the normal rush hour exodus except that everyone was streaming away from chaos rather than the mundane routine of their 9 to 5 jobs.

They walked up Pine and decided to stop at Kincora Pub for a pint of Guinness, where they sat down and watched the big screen television with the rest of the people in the bar as downtown melted even further into mayhem. More tear gas was dispersed, flash bombs were exploding, dumpsters were being rolled, people were running, and police were giving chase. Many windows were broken and small fires burned in almost every garbage can.

They watched in silence as the chaos snowballed at the corner where the three of them had just been standing. Groups of protestors were now taking on the police in block-to-block skirmishes. A crowd of people stood outside the bar and looked through the window to see what was happening on the television. Others arrived from downtown with firsthand reports about what was taking place on the screen just blocks away.

Jack went to a payphone outside and checked his messages. His brother was at The Elysian with Eve having dinner. They watched for another half hour as downtown Seattle was transformed into a battle zone. Helicopters hovered overhead, shining their spotlights down on the city. When they got to the Elysian, everyone there was gathered around the bar's lone television. The situation downtown had descended further still into chaos.

The police were now chasing people up the hill, across the I-5 bridge and onto Capitol Hill. The air outside the Bauhaus was thick with tear gas. Jack ordered a beer, a small salad, and fish and chips, and leaned back into his seat to watch as the battle moved up into his neighborhood. The bartender declared it Happy Hour for the rest of the night and everyone in the bar cheered. Needless to say, they ordered another round.

The police moved further up into Capitol Hill, lobbing tear gas and concussion grenades as they went. They were now next to the Cha Cha Lounge and Bimbo's Bitchin' Burrito Kitchen on Pine. Jack and his friends paid their bill and walked down the hill to get a closer look at the action. At the corner of 12th and Pike, he looked up to see a karate class in progress in a window as a huge cloud of tear gas rose into the sky several blocks away.

A crowd had gathered and formed a line at the corner of Broadway and Pine. They assembled a barricade in front of the Egyptian Theatre with dumpsters taken from the alley and newspaper vending machines from the sidewalk. They taunted and yelled profanities at the police, who had formed a line of their own in front of the Hi-Score Arcade, where they stood massed behind an armored car.

Jack walked down to Linda's and looked in at everybody drinking inside. People were gathered near the windows, pints in hand, looking down the street and waiting to see what was going to happen next. Others were just sitting and talking, seemingly oblivious to what was going on. A few people were shooting pool.

He walked down the street to get a closer look at the armored car and the faceless riot police standing around it. People looked down from above inside their apartments on either side of the street. The air was filled with the scent of tear gas and the noise of the hovering helicopter. The scene was surreal. Why had they come so far from into Capitol Hill? They had succeeded in driving the protestors and hooligans from downtown. What were they trying to do now?

Jack walked back up the hill, took another look at the crowd behind the barrier, and decided to go to the Bad Juju Lounge for a nightcap with a couple friends he found at Linda's. He was starting to feel tired. He was aware that he had quaffed a fair share of beer throughout the day, but the adrenaline pumping through his veins and the mood in the air seemed to have negated the effects of the alcohol. Jack was disappointed that the staff at the Bad Juju did not have their television tuned into the goings on, but figured that maybe things were winding down by then anyway.

In the midst of their conversation, fifteen police cars with lights flashing and sirens blaring appeared on the street in front of the bar. Each car was filled with four or five policemen in full riot gear. The Bad Juju Lounge staff closed their curtains. Jack decided it was time to go home and get some rest. He had been up and on his feet since six in the morning and his body was starting to feel it. He said good night to his friends and left the bar.

As he walked towards Pine, a squad of riot police marched by and headed towards Broadway. He had chosen a rather inappropriate time to leave. He reached the sidewalk and turned to the left to follow them and see what was happening now. Another squad of riot police was marching down from the precinct. Jack was in between the two squads. Police cars and vans arrived with their sirens blaring and handfuls of riot police spilled out of each. There were now several hundred marching down to disperse the crowd. Jack watched as the police shot tear gas and concussion grenades down Broadway in front of the Seattle Central Community College campus. He decided to walk down 11th and over to Broadway via Denny to watch what was unfolding. He heard more explosions as he walked in the rain past the reservoir.

When he got to Broadway next to the Bonney Watson Funeral Home parking lot, a wave of tear gas passed over and for the first time he felt the pain of its sting. This pain did not last very long, though, as the cloud of gas had dispersed considerably by the time it reached him. Still, he made a mental note in his mind that he had just been tear-gassed for the first time. He looked down Broadway and saw the police in a line across the street near the Seattle Central bookstore. Every now and then they shot a tear gas canister towards the crowd, which now included protestors as well as people from the neighborhood going about their business but now caught up in the action.

Jack decided again that it was time to head home, but instead walked past Denny, which was the fastest way to get to his apartment, and stood in front of Jack In The Box to check out the crowd gathered in the parking lot at Dick's across the street. The combination of tear gas and hamburger meat cooking made for a unique aroma.

As he stood there, a young man driving slowly down Broadway hit a young woman who was crossing the street. She had been running and slowed down almost to a walk when he drove by looking to his left, then hit his gas pedal, speeding up and striking her lower leg and foot with his bumper. The woman spun around like a ballerina and cried out in pain. The guy who hit her stopped his car and got out to see if she was okay.

She limped to the curb and sat down as the driver leaned down to try to comfort her. As he did, a guy dressed in a black hoodie and black mask ran into the street, jumped into the car, put it into gear, and sped off down the street.

"Dude, someone's stealing your car!" Jack yelled.

The owner of the car turned away from the young woman and ran after it. The guy behind the wheel gunned the engine, cut into the Jack In The Box parking lot, and disappeared up Denny and into the night.

While this was happening, a group of teenagers worked at setting fire to the contents of two dumpsters they had taken from the Kinko's parking lot on the other corner of Denny and Broadway.

A man yelled at them from his apartment window above, "Why don't you go and destroy your own neighborhood! Why are you doing this up here?"

The group shouted obscenities at him and he threatened to bring out his gun. Another group of people stood near Jack drinking beer and watching what was happening with amused looks on their faces.

Now it really was a good time to go home, Jack thought. There was no rule of law on the streets, just a truly dangerous form of chaos. Finally at home, Jack took off his shoes, turned off the lights, and got into bed. A helicopter circled overhead and sirens filled the air.

Images from the day passed through his mind as he drifted off to sleep.

DECEMBER 1, 1999: WEDNESDAY

As soon as Jack woke up in the morning, he turned on the television. A state of civil emergency had been declared, the National Guard was being called in, and a "No Protest Zone" had been established downtown.

Jack watched as a small group of protestors assembled and began to march towards downtown. A squad of riot police followed. He recognized them as the same squad that had marched past him the night before at the Bad Juju Lounge. They had been up all night.

A half hour later, the cameras captured the action as the protestors were blocked from advancing into the downtown area and were rounded up and arrested on the spot. The reporters on the scene said that the police descended on the protestors and confiscated their banners and signs because they could be used as weapons.

A news helicopter hovered over the National Guard Armory in Kent and filmed a Guard unit as it mobilized. Jack watched as the convoy made its way onto the highway and headed towards downtown to help restore order.

At 1:00, he decided to walk downtown and take some pictures in the "No Protest Zone." Riot police were stationed on the bridge near the Paramount Theatre, where he was directed a block over if he wanted to go downtown, which appeared to be deserted. Windows were boarded up and stores and restaurants were closed. National Guard troops and riot police in full riot gear were stationed on every corner and all of them held long wooden batons.

Most of the National Guard troops looked like they were in their early twenties. Jack wondered how many of them had ever imagined they would be keeping the peace in downtown Seattle one day. He took a few pictures and walked around to look at the damage. The Starbucks that was trashed the day before was boarded shut.

At the corner across from the Sheraton Hotel parking lot, he watched as a British news reporter flubbed his lines for the camera several times before finally getting through his report on the chaos on Seattle's streets while W.T.O. delegates arrived to attend the conference.

Two drunks were told by one of the sheriffs to hand over their forty-ounce bottles of beer and leave the area. A leather-faced older sheriff poured the beer out onto the street, looked at Jack, smiling, and asked: "Want some?"

The air was cold and damp. He was shivering and wished that he had put on another layer when he left his apartment. He walked up the street towards the Holiday Inn. A line of police let him pass, but they didn't let him walk back when he decided he wanted to return to the corner where he was just standing, so he walked back towards downtown to take a few more pictures and find a different way up the hill to his neighborhood.

The scene was the same everywhere: National Guard troops and riot police on every corner. There was no evidence of any protest groups anywhere in sight. There was still tension in the air, but it was a rather boring tension, as nothing was happening.

He stopped in at a Chinese restaurant to eat a late lunch and was one of only three customers. As he ate, Jack read the paper while a radio journalist on NPR talked about the ethnic cleansing in Rwanda a few years earlier.

When he finished eating, it was close to 4:00. He walked down the street towards the Westlake Center and turned left towards the Pike Place Market. He wasn't sure where he was going. The police lines seemed to have different rules from block to block, so to get back to Capitol Hill it looked like he was going to have to walk all the way around the downtown core to get to a street he could use to walk towards home.

He figured his best bet would be Pine and the bridge over the I-5. If that didn't work, he would walk over to Denny and cross there. As he walked, he heard someone mention that tear gas was being used around the corner somewhere down on 1st or 2nd Ave, but there weren't any sirens in the air and everything seemed quiet. There were enough people walking around near 1st Ave going about their business to give the appearance that it was just another regular day.

As he crossed 2nd Ave., he looked down the street and saw people moving quickly in his direction holding their hands over their mouths and eyes. He didn't see a cloud of tear gas in the air so he wasn't sure what was going on, but as he crossed the street and stood in front of the Nordstrom Rack, he realized that he was going to be downwind of whatever was blowing towards him and was suddenly overcome. He squinted his stinging eyes tightly and turned to run down the street.

When he opened his mouth to breathe, the back of his throat felt like he had swallowed gasoline. Tears ran down his face. He couldn't think straight and was gasping for breath. He saw a group of people push their way into an apartment lobby after a security guard had opened the door so they could get away from the gas. He stumbled into the lobby and leaned against the wall with the group of strangers who were also gasping for breath, rubbing their eyes, moaning, and swearing.

A few teenagers lay down on the floor in front of the elevators and rolled around in agony. Nobody spoke. Everyone was involved in his or her own pain. It was a strange scene. Jack wondered who they all were. It was obvious that not one of them was a protestor. There were men and women in business clothes, people with shopping bags, senior citizens, and teenagers. More people knocked desperately on the glass door and begged the security guard to let them in.

When he opened the door again, Jack felt recovered enough to head back out to the street. He heard someone say that something was going on at the Pike Place Market and walked to 1st Ave. When he arrived at the top of the hill above the market, vans and cars full of riot police were dropping off their passengers. An armored car pulled up with riot police sitting on its top and sides pointing their rubber bullet and tear gas guns at those on the sidewalk.

Curious bystanders following the proceedings crossed paths with people who were just trying to get home from work for the night who looked confused and scared. The armored vehicle moved down the hill towards the Pike Place Market with what appeared to be nearly a hundred riot police marching behind.

Six explosions echoed against the buildings and a huge cloud of tear gas rose into the sky. Jack continued to be pulled along with the crowd that was now gathering more and more people as it moved forward. He kept track of where he was in relation to the police and the denser parts of the crowd to keep an avenue of escape open.

Shop and restaurant employees stood in their windows and watched as the action passed by. Waiters and a couple chefs stood with their arms folded across their chests inside Lampreia. Jack didn't see anyone eating dinner inside.

The armored car zipped down a side street. He ran another block or two so that he could stand at a distance and watch what was happening. He was near Minnie's in lower Queen Anne when he heard a series of explosions from the next block over. When he turned the corner, he saw that the police had a group of protestors boxed in. They had moved in from both ends of 1st Ave and pushed them onto the sidewalk in front of an apartment building.

There were probably a hundred protestors. The police yelled for them to sit down, all the time pointing their rubber bullet guns at them. Jack looked up at the apartment building and saw people standing in their windows. As the protestors sat on the ground, two Metro buses arrived to take them away.

The police handcuffed each person with plastic ties and walked them to the bus. After a while, he got tired of watching the protestors being put on the bus and decided that it was time to head back downtown to try to get back to Capitol Hill.

When he got back to the downtown core, something weird was happening. Dozens of police cars were driving in circles around the block with their sirens on. They circled around one block and then came to a halt in the middle of the intersection with their sirens blaring and lights flashing.

An armored vehicle drove by and the riot police hanging onto its side looked everyone on the sidewalks in the eye as they passed. News crews arrived on the scene and a crowd of onlookers gathered at the corner of 3rd and Pine in front of McDonald's.

Police cars continued to arrive from all directions. Jack crossed the street and stood on the corner as a line of riot police moved towards him. He turned to walk away and watched in horror as another group of riot police got out of their van and formed a line in front of him. He was boxed in. He turned and ran across the street while others stayed behind. The police boxed them in and yelled at them to leave the area. Jack saw a clock and realized that in less than a half hour he would be standing inside the curfew zone where he would be subject to arrest.

He asked an officer sitting in a patrol car how he could get back up to Capitol Hill, but he just shrugged and pointed in the other direction. Jack asked him what was going on. He said he had no idea. Jack would learn later that this police tactic of arriving on the scene and stirring up a ruckus was called "The Weasel." It was a maneuver meant to clear people out of the area.

A group of protestors formed a circle in the middle of the intersection in front of McDonald's at 3rd and Pine. It was now fifteen minutes before 7:00. Jack overheard a National Guard sergeant tell a group of people that they were in the curfew zone and that in fifteen minutes they would be in danger of being arrested.

A sheriff's deputy walked over and told those who were standing there that it would be wise to leave the area as police were planning to use more tear gas soon. She escorted a drunk around the corner and told him to sit down on the ground because he would get hurt if he walked in the other direction towards the crowd and the imminent gassing of the protestors. Jack walked in front of one of the news cameras and was later told by one of his friends that he had appeared on live television.

He walked up Pine towards Capitol Hill, crossed the highway, and walked past the Bauhaus coffee shop, picturing the scenes he had seen unfold on the news the night before. He walked past the Kincora. The pub was again filled with people watching the latest developments unfold on their big screen television.

It looked like a busy night on Broadway with lots of people walking around, shopping, and eating dinner in restaurants, and he briefly considered hanging around for a while. Sometimes walking down Broadway made him feel like he was living in a big and bustling city. He had grown weary, though, from two long days in a row, and decided to go home. His feet hurt and he was cold. It was time to eat a good meal and get some rest.

He went home, took off his shoes, and turned on the news. The police had cleared downtown of protestors and anyone who was still there when the curfew went into effect at 7 p.m. A large group of protestors walked up Denny towards Capitol Hill with a group of police behind them to make sure they kept walking away from the downtown area.

The news reporter said that they planned to assemble on the corner of Broadway and Pine near Seattle Central Community College. Sirens and the sound of the police helicopter filled the air again outside his window. It was a crisp, cold night. The air was fresh, but he still had a lingering taste of tear gas in his mouth and his clothes reeked from being gassed a few hours earlier.

At some point, all three news stations returned to their regularly scheduled programs and Jack turned off the TV. The protestors were just a few blocks away from Broadway before the news stations cut away. It seemed strange that they were not going to continue to follow their movement up to Capitol Hill. He lay back down on his bed and called his ex-girlfriend upstairs to chat about everything that had been going on. He wondered if her new guy was there, listening to their conversation the way he had listened to her conversations with her friends when they still lived together.

While they were talking, explosions filled the air from Broadway and the Seattle Central campus. First one volley, then another, followed by yet one more. He told his ex that he was going to go and see what was going on. After he hung up the phone, he grabbed his coat and a dishtowel from the kitchen to cover his nose and mouth and ran out into the night towards Broadway and the sounds of explosions and screams.

The streets were wet and slippery. The sky lit up with white light after each concussion grenade exploded. When he reached the reservoir, he slowed down to a walk and watched through the gap between buildings as an army of riot police moved slowly from left to right through a cloud of tear gas. They appeared to be firing and throwing tear gas and concussion grenades as they walked.

He ran down Denny towards the Vivace coffee shop and Jack In The Box to try to get a better look. He thought the police would push the protestors to the corner and create a line like he had seen them do the past two days. He stopped at the corner of 10th and Denny and watched in disbelief as the riot police marched into the intersection and lobbed concussion grenades and tear gas in both directions up and down Denny.

He saw something flying through the air in his direction and turned and ran down 10th. He looked behind him over his shoulder as a concussion grenade exploded in the air just fifty feet away. He also heard the hiss of a tear gas canister going off in the street. His eyes began to water, so he pulled his dishtowel out to hold over his mouth as he ran.

Again he wanted to get ahead of the action so that he could watch it from a safe distance, but as he ran the police continued to advance down Broadway. He heard more explosions and saw a tear gas projectile fly through the air high above Broadway and the buildings he was running parallel to. People were running both away from Broadway and towards it, some trying to get away from the action while others were trying to get a better look. He ran as fast as he could to the corner of 10th and John, crossed the street near the Mystery Soda machine and began to walk towards Broadway.

Again, he thought the police were going to draw a line, and again he was not fast enough to get ahead of them. He made it to about fifty feet from the corner when the riot police reached the crosswalk.

They fired more tear gas canisters down the street in front of them and, as they went through the intersection, they hurled concussion grenades and tear gas canisters to the sides as well. Jack coughed as a thin cloud of tear gas blew over him. He turned to run with the people running towards him trying to get away.

It was hard to believe the police were going right down Broadway, especially since it was such a busy night with the streets filled with people going about their business at the end of the day.

Again he ran down 10th parallel to Broadway then tried to cut up towards Ileen's. Again, he couldn't get ahead of the police. They were moving too fast and weren't stopping. They continued to throw grenades and tear gas down every side street and straight ahead down Broadway. Crowds of people streamed down from the neighborhood to see what was going on.

There were kids in black outfits in the shadows of the side street with scarves covering their faces. Jack slowed down every now and then when he reached a corner to look and see if he could see what was happening, but on each corner it was the same: more tear gas and more concussion grenades. There appeared to be hundreds of riot police on Broadway.

Near the Safeway parking lot, he watched as a cloud of gas blew towards him. He turned, ducked, and held his towel up to his face, but it didn't do any good. Again, he got a good painful whiff. It didn't seem to matter if you were holding your breath or covering your face. The gas still got into your eyes and your nose.

A few people in the crowd wore gas masks, which, he heard on the news, had been declared illegal in the city and could be punished with a $500 fine. People continued to come down from their houses and apartments on either side of Broadway to see what was going on. Everyone had towels to hold over their mouths, and some had bottles of water to pour on their eyes if they were gassed.

Jack stood behind a light post near the gas station across from The Deluxe and watched as an armored car took up a position in the intersection. A pair of riot police stood on either side and faced the people who stood and stared back at them. A riot policeman on the armored car pointed its spotlight at them and the police helicopter flew overhead and shined its spotlight up and down Broadway.

Jack crossed the street and stood in front of The Deluxe with the crowd that was gathering there. There were couples old and young that looked like they were out for an evening stroll. A teenage kid chanted, seemingly to no one in particular, "The crazy weed, the crazy weed!"

Every minute or so, there was another concussion grenade explosion and more tear gas. A few people yelled at the police to get out of the neighborhood. There appeared to be riot police all the way down Broadway.

Jack had looked down at this exact corner just four nights earlier from the plane. He couldn't have imagined that he would be standing there seeing what he was seeing unfold in front of him. He walked back over to 10th, keeping an eye on the riot police and the armored car behind him just in case they decided to attack, and slowly made his way back to the Safeway parking lot on Broadway. He watched as the police slowly started to retreat down the street and people walked behind. As they retreated, they shot off more concussion grenades and tear gas behind them.

People were yelling now: "Off Our Hill! Off Our Hill!"

Block by block, the police continued to pull back. The crowd snowballed in size as people came out from the side streets to join in.

"Off Our Hill! Off Our Hill!"

More explosions. More tear gas. Jack looked into restaurant and coffee shop windows as he walked. Every window was filled with shocked faces. The windows at Ileen's were filled with people looking out and sipping their drinks. A window table at Ileen's had probably never offered up a more surreal scene.

The crowd was growing in size. He returned to the dark safety of 10th and made his way towards Seattle Central, where everyone seemed to be moving. In front of the funeral home, he watched as a riot policeman shot rubber bullets at a man standing on the sidewalk just a few feet away. A motion in the crowd of riot police created a panic and all the people turned and ran down the side street where Jack was standing. He turned and ran himself until the panic ebbed and people returned to Broadway. Those sudden panics could get you trampled, Jack thought.

He walked down Federal to the reservoir. An armored car drove towards him. He hopped the embankment and moved into the dark of the park. The police continued their retreat to the precinct on 12th and Pine, where they formed a line with riot police, squad cars, and an armored car, its spotlight pointed at the crowd that had grown to a thousand people or more extending to the corner of Broadway and Pine, everyone chanting, "Off Our Hill! Off Our Hill!"

A limousine appeared and tried to move through the intersection. Some in the crowd, perhaps thinking that it contained a dignitary from the W.T.O., pounded on its hood and threw bottles at it as it passed. Some kids in black hoodies began to pull bricks up from the sidewalk and piled them into stacks the way kids piled snowballs for snowball fights. Jack stood beneath the trees on the hill across from the Egyptian Theatre and waited to see what was going to happen next. It felt like they were waiting for a concert to start. A festival atmosphere filled the air again. People with drums arrived on the scene and began to play. The police helicopter circled overhead. He crossed the street and stood in the AEI parking lot to look across the field towards the police precinct. Some in the crowd walked right up to within twenty or thirty feet of the police line to yell at them for what had happened on Broadway.

The stretch of Pine Street near Kentucky Fried Chicken began to fill up as more and more people moved towards the police line. The police shot a few tear gas canisters and concussion grenades into the crowd to try to disperse them, but this only angered them and after each volley they continued to advance.

The police helicopter disappeared for what seemed like fifteen or twenty minutes, probably to refuel somewhere before it returned to circle and shine its light down on the crowd. The police shot off another volley of tear gas and concussion grenades. The helicopter spotlight in the cloud of gas was an eerie, beautiful sight. Jack watched as the beautiful cloud wafted over the field towards him and was quickly doubled up in pain next to two guys wearing gas masks watching the proceedings.

It seemed to be a stronger type of gas and felt more like a liquid that stuck to his skin and got inside his pores. One of the guys asked if he was okay as he coughed and dabbed his eyes.

Tear gas is like heartbreak. You know what to expect when it's on the way but it hurts just the same every time.

"You know," Jack said dryly, after the pain from the gas had gone away, "You guys can get fined five hundred dollars for wearing those things." They laughed inside their masks.

After each volley, some in the crowd ran forward to collect souvenirs, which made Jack think that he wanted a souvenir too. A few minutes later, after the police shot a few rounds of tear gas onto the field, he ran over and picked one up with his dishtowel. It was scalding hot. He watched as it hissed and spewed out the remainder of its gas. This was milder than the other gas. It was still unpleasant, but tolerable. He rubbed the cartridge in the wet grass to cool it down and put it in his pocket. He noticed that some of the other souvenir collectors in the crowd had picked up the really big tear gas projectiles and he wanted one of those as well. Suddenly he had become a collector.

Standing under a tree near the sidewalk, he struck up a conversation with a guy who lived in the neighborhood and had witnessed riots in Europe. He seemed to be enjoying himself and they exchanged stories about the evening. Jack mentioned how he felt like he had suddenly become a collector. The guy pulled a brown paper bag from his coat pocket and showed Jack the spent tear gas projectile he was hoping to find.

"Damn," he said, "I want one of those, all I have are these."

Jack showed him the three tear gas cartridges he had picked up along with a few of the concussion grenade pellets and the guy lamented the fact that he didn't have more than one of the gas canisters that he might trade. They talked for a while longer until he said that he was going to go to the other side of the street because he felt like he would have a better escape route from there if anything were to happen.

"Good luck," Jack said, and watched him disappear into the crowd. A punk rocker dressed in black leather with spiked hair stopped in front of Jack and said, in a thick English accent, "They're using different *levels* of gas, do you know what I mean? Different *levels*."

The helicopter flew off again. It seemed that when the helicopter disappeared, the action on the ground stopped. Each time it returned, though, the pattern was the same. It circled overhead for a few minutes, shining its spotlight down on the area. Soon after, the riot police attacked and tried again to disperse the crowd.

It felt like a street party now. People were playing drums and dancing, laughing and talking about things unrelated to what was going on. It was a street party except for the fact that several hundred police in full combat gear were watching over the proceedings from a block away, with hundreds more garrisoned and waiting for orders inside the precinct.

Jack ran into Curtis sitting on his bike next to the tree where he had been standing earlier. He was at home when he heard what was going on and had gotten dressed and headed out into the night to see for himself.

They agreed that they had lost track of their everyday responsibilities. Jack described some of the scenes he had witnessed and listened to Curtis's stories. They waited for the next attack, and when the police helicopter returned he told Curtis that it wouldn't be long now.

Eventually, though, an hour passed without anything happening. People had grown brave enough to walk right up next to the police line to stare curiously at the officers and the National Guard. A half hour later, Curtis decided that he was tired and ready to go home. Jack said he only had ten or fifteen minutes left in his tank.

Curtis rode his bike into the night and Jack stood off to the side of the main police line waiting to see if anything was going to happen. He realized then how cold he was after standing there in the rain for four hours. He turned and headed towards home.

Once inside, he took his shoes off and lay down on his bed. Three or four minutes passed as he let his mind wander over the images of the day, and just as he was beginning to take the first step towards a solid sleep, he heard explosions and screams coming from the line a few blocks away. He listened as they echoed into the night and drifted to sleep with the sound of the helicopter circling in the sky overhead.

DECEMBER 2, 1999: THURSDAY

Jack woke up feeling tense and in a heightened state of readiness for whatever was going to happen. After only just two days immersed in the chaos, he had already taken for granted that it was going to continue. He walked around Broadway and 11th to look for leftover riot souvenirs from the night before. On the ground next to a trashcan there were two large boxes filled with the cardboard tubes the large tear gas containers had been stored in. He tore the box top off to keep as a souvenir, continued to wander, and picked up nearly a hundred rubber pellets from the ground.

After he was finished gathering souvenirs, he took himself out to lunch and read both *The Seattle Times* and *P-I's* coverage of the previous day's events.

He puttered around his apartment for a while and lay down to take a nap around 5:00. When he woke up at 6:30, he turned on the news and saw that people were gathering at Seattle Central Community College to protest the police actions on Capitol Hill.

He grabbed his dishtowel on the way out, expecting to have to use it against the tear gas he was sure would be used again. When he reached Broadway, the crowd was walking in double file down the sidewalk, chanting, "Whose streets? Our streets! Whose streets? Our streets!"

He saw his friend Jason walking with his bicycle. They exchanged stories from the last few days and walked along with the crowd to the end of Broadway and The Deluxe, where they crossed the street and headed back in the direction from which they had come, just as the police had advanced and retreated the night before.

People in passing cars honked and raised their fists and flashed the peace sign as they passed. People sitting in restaurants and coffee shops also smiled as they walked by.

Quite a few businesses were closed for the night, their owners probably expecting more violence. As they walked, though, there was a feeling of deflation in the air, and when they got back to Seattle Central and assembled where all the news vans were parked near the South Plaza, Jack had a feeling that it was all over, that after what had happened the day before there would be no more chaos and no more tear gas.

He didn't have it in him to go through another night of similar activity and wondered if perhaps everyone in town was feeling the same weariness and that it was time to get some rest and let life return to its normal lethargic pace.

A massive group of protestors arrived from downtown, where they had been staging a rally and protest demanding the release of the hundreds of people who had been arrested over the past two days. They were escorted by motorcycle police and not met this time by police in riot gear on Broadway.

Jason and Jack went to an art opening at the Houston gallery and drank a few beers. Jack kept picturing scenes from the night before when he looked out the window and couldn't believe that it was just twenty-four hours earlier that the chaos had unfolded. They left the gallery and decided to go down to Pioneer Square and The O.K. Hotel, where Ota Prota and The Anti-Fascist Marching Band were playing a benefit for Free Seattle Radio.

They walked down Pine towards I-5 and observed the police line for a few minutes near the Paramount Theatre. Earlier in the day, Jack heard on the radio that if you had "legitimate business" you were allowed to pass through the No Protest Zone. Oddly, "legitimate business" included going to a club for a show.

He walked up to one of the riot police to ask him how they should proceed downtown. When he first approached him, Jack saw him tense up in anticipation of their interaction, but when he asked him what he thought the best way to get through downtown was, the officer seemed to relax and appeared relieved to point them one street over.

The police helicopter hovered overhead. A few stray troublemakers were trying to get something started with the single line of riot police. Others, though, were asking to have their pictures taken with the officers, who seemed amused and agreed to be photographed.

Jason and Jack walked a street over and continued on their way downtown. They came across a parked squad car, four handcuffed youths sitting on the curb, and a single police officer standing to the side, perhaps waiting for backup. Jack approached him and asked which way they should proceed to get to Pioneer Square.

"That's *your* path," he said, stoically. Jack pressed him for details, asking if it would be okay to walk down this or that street and again he said, this time with fatigue in his voice, "It's your path."

As they walked away and discussed what he meant, Jack and Jason decided that he was saying they could walk wherever they wanted to and that he too was tired of dealing with the whole thing. It *was* their path.

Perhaps the No Protest Zone tonight was just an illusion to keep people off the streets. There were still police and National Guard posted at corners around the Convention Center where the conference was going on, but they were not arresting people or chasing them away.

Downtown was deserted, though, so even if it was an illusion, it was an effective illusion.

They walked by the Lusty Lady and laughed at the sign on its marquee: "W.T. Oooooooh!"

The O.K. Hotel was packed. Everyone was partying and in a good mood. A few of the Santa Eleven were there, but only two were in costume. Ota Prota was onstage playing their song "The Idiot." They played like they were out of their minds.

Everyone in the club seemed to be out of their minds too. The week's events had left people feeling a combination of adrenaline-driven euphoria and fatigue, and now they were both tired and drunk. At midnight, Jack's friend Nicholas found out it was his birthday.

"Tequila!" he yelled to the bartender.

As soon as the shots were headed his way, Jack knew that it was not the kind of trouble he was looking for, but there was nothing he could do. You can't turn down a birthday shot. He tossed his shot back and waited for its effects to kick in. Sure enough, he found himself quickly feeling sloppy drunk and watched as the room began to melt and fold in on itself.

He said good night to everyone and ambled out into the street, where he walked up the hill, across the I-5 bridge, through First Hill, down Broadway, and up to his apartment.

"Fuckin' Nicholas," he mumbled as he climbed under the covers. "Fuckin' tequila."

DECEMBER 3, 1999: FRIDAY

Jack woke up the next morning to the sound of the phone ringing. He answered and listened with a half smile, half hung over grimace as his parents sang "Happy Birthday."

It was his birthday, but throughout the day he kept it to himself. It felt like one of those birthdays it was better not to celebrate. Things had been different a year ago. His girlfriend and he were still together and things hadn't yet started to fall apart.

He walked down Broadway all the way up to The Deluxe and found two hundred rubber pellets. He noticed a few other people also scanning the ground for souvenirs.

By now, he had a pretty good collection of riot junk going: rubber pellets, rubber bullets, tear gas cartridges, pins from tear gas or concussion grenades, and pieces of the black rubber concussion grenade casings.

Near Broadway and John, he found pieces of the grenade that had been thrown in his direction two nights earlier.

Jack's ex-girlfriend called in the afternoon and offered to take him out to dinner. They met and at Hopscotch on 15th. He listened for hints about what was going on between her and the new guy.

She said that it was nothing serious, which made Jack feel hopeful for a moment that maybe they could patch things up at some point.

After dinner, he asked about her plans for the rest of the night. She said she was going to meet some friends at

Charlie's to shoot some pool. He gave her a little gift box, inside of which he had placed a selection of some of his hard-earned riot souvenirs.

He felt relieved that she wasn't going to meet the new guy. They walked down to Broadway together and hugged before going their separate ways. He watched as she walked towards Charlie's and after she disappeared inside, he went to Ileen's to have a beer.

Later, after deciding to see some of his friends for a birthday drink, he sat at the bar in Linda's and tried not feel too sorry for himself.

He looked at the clock. There were only ten minutes of birthday left. He decided to call it a night.

When he turned the corner at Denny and Broadway, there just fifty feet in front of him was his ex-girlfriend holding hands with her new guy as they walked up the hill.

Jack realized that she had said she was meeting friends to spare him from being unhappy on his birthday, but his heart sank. Since they lived in the same building, there was no choice but to walk slowly behind them.

In her free hand was the gift box he had given her. Jack watched as they entered their building and waited on the corner for a minute before going in so as to avoid running into them in the lobby.

Once inside, he fell on the bed in a defeated heap.

Not much of a birthday, he thought, but quite a week.

AFTERMATH

It was over. Jack was nostalgic for yesterday, nostalgic for the night before, nostalgic for the beautiful chaos that had unfolded during the week, nostalgic for the mood on the street, the feeling in the air, the smell and taste of tear gas, and the possibility, fleeting as it was, that anything was possible, and that manifestations of that possibility had appeared all over town.

He was exhausted, though, and knew that even though his mind wanted to experience more chaos, it was time for his body to get some rest and reset its clock back to the humdrum everyday routine.

When you expect anything to happen, nothing is surprising, he thought, picturing the moment the previous week when, dressed as Santa Claus, he watched as the black limousine drove into the intersection at 4th and Pine and the police leaped out of their unmarked vehicle with M-16s at the ready.

Thinking back on that moment, it was hard to imagine how nonchalant he felt about what was happening in front of him. The limousine being blocked in the intersection simply made sense in the moment. The sound of one of its windows being smashed was more expected than surprising, and when the police got out of their vehicle with M-16's equipped with laser sights, he did not think about the danger of being shot, he only noted how quickly they had arrived.

A week later, he had grown tired of talking about it. Everyone had his or her own story to tell, and everyone wanted to tell it.

It felt like they had all seen the same movie. How long, how many times, can you talk about your favorite scenes before doing so wears thin?

It is inconceivable, in retrospect, to think that in the midst of all that chaos not one person died, and though numerous people were injured, the whole week was ultimately, in a way, a combination of spectacle and live theatre.

At the same time, all that separated the city from the potential outbreak of *true* chaos was death. A single death would have provided the spark to an even more unimaginable outcome that might have plunged the city into a darkness so complete that everyone's perception of the week's reality would be much different for years after.

The media and police labeled the people who were downtown as protestors and anarchists, but there was no mention of the thousands who were simply there, like Jack, to bear witness.

He discovered in the weeks after that he had little to talk about with people who were not in the least bit curious to know what happened that week.

He discovered that he had little to talk about with people who didn't appreciate the beauty of the crowd of strangers who had joined together to experience such unsupervised and unscripted spectacle.

The people he could relate to the most were those who understood that it had been a party, pure and simple, and that something important happened in the midst of that party.

It was hard to feel sorry for Mayor Schell and those in charge of creating a safe environment that would allow the conference to take place and the protestors to have their say.

If Jack suspected the week was going to lead to the kinds of events it did, and if the mayor of Seattle did not, did that make him smarter than the mayor?

The only information Jack had was what he read in the newspapers, and just from reading about it, he knew there was going to be trouble. No one could have imagined, though, how unprepared the city was to deal with that trouble once it began.

Everyone involved played their part to the tee and all deserved equal recognition for a spectacle that was well played out to a worldwide audience.

Life, a few weeks later, had returned to its normal state of lethargy and routine. Everyone Jack talked to who was there spoke with a glint in their eyes when they talked about what they saw that week.

Everyone who was there understood the fine line that existed between the everyday world and the world of chaos and looming just on the other side of its rules and boundaries.

Jack could still hear the sirens and the explosions of the concussion grenades, the yells and cheers of the people in the street. He could still hear the helicopter in the sky as it circled overhead. He could still taste and smell the tear gas in the air.

For weeks after, the sound of sirens and helicopters made him pause whatever he was doing in anticipation of chaos to follow.

The chaos had settled for now, but it was still there, just beneath the surface, waiting for the next flash point to arrive to rear its ugly, beautiful head.

SEATTLE STORIES (THE '90s)

WORLD & NEEDLE

As the train slowly wound its way along the water towards its final destination, Jack stared out the window and wondered what his life in Seattle would be like. He had no clear plan, little money, and only vague offers of couches to sleep on from his brother and a couple friends who had moved there ahead of him.

After passing through the train yards beneath Queen Anne Hill, the city revealed itself in the form of a glimpse of the rotating globe on top of the *Seattle Post-Intelligencer* newspaper building and the Space Needle standing as if in welcome beyond.

The globe glowed brightly against the late afternoon overcast sky and seemed to Jack to be a promising symbol of what the city might have to offer. The Space Needle appeared to be a knowing sentinel, though it gave no hint about the content of its knowledge.

The train pulled into the station. Jack stepped onto the platform, took a deep breath of the damp and slightly salty air, and moved away from the train with the rest of the passengers towards the doors to the city.

WILD BILL

Wild Bill was a friend of Jack's friend Virginia and an electrician in the film industry. When Jack met him he had last worked on Oliver Stone's *Natural Born Killers* and was in Seattle to work on *Mad Love* with Drew Barrymore.

Wild Bill wanted a taste of the nightlife, so Krantz, Virginia, and Jack took him downtown. While talking to him on the way to the club, Jack quickly realized that Seattle might prove to be too tame a town for Wild Bill's liking.

Wild Bill lived in the New Mexico desert. He worked only part of each year on one or two films to make enough money to go off on his own adventures. For Wild Bill, life was action.

As they walked, Wild Bill talked about his love of riding motorcycles a hundred and fifty miles an hour on the highway. Jack asked him if he was ever afraid of getting into an accident.

"Not at all," Wild Bill said. "When you're moving that fast everyone else looks like they're standing still. You have full control. They don't even notice you pass them by."

Wild Bill said he put away about an ounce of marijuana a day. He said he had been electrocuted a few times while working on film sets and that doctors had detected an extra blip in his heartbeat.

He described years of living off the ocean with the indigenous population of some South Pacific island. When Jack asked him how he spent his time there, Wild Bill looked at him as if the answer to his question was obvious.

"You know," he said, "the hunt. Every day, thirty men in boats, paddle out to sea, paddle back with food for the village." The film company had rented out a floor of downtown suites for the crew in the apartment tower next to The Paramount Theatre. The next day after lunch, Wild Bill told Jack and Krantz to come to his suite later in the afternoon for "a feast" and took Virginia to the Pike Place Market to gather everything he needed for the meal.

Jack went back to the apartment to take a nap and ponder the matter of the vial of psilocybin from New Mexico that Wild Bill had in his possession. Part of "the feast" was to include the ingestion of a healthy dose of shroom dust before heading out into the night.

The Fear welled up inside Jack's mind. It had been years since he had last tripped and that last trip had taught him that he probably shouldn't trip again.

"I don't know if I should shroom," Jack said to Wild Bill.

Wild Bill replied, emphatically: "You *do*."

Jack put a blanket over his head and fell into a brief but restful stupor. When he woke, it was time to go to the feast. He met Krantz in front of the building and they rode the elevator up to the suite.

When Wild Bill opened the door and welcomed them inside, it was evident that in the last two hours he hadn't had time for nor did he need anything resembling a nap.

He had been busy preparing the feast and was amazed at the things he'd found at the market, where he had spent hundreds of dollars on the meal the four of them would soon enjoy.

While he worked in the kitchen, Jack, Krantz and Virginia drank beers and looked out at the view. They packed and smoked a fat bowl of kind bud, after which Wild Bill announced it was time to start the feast.

On the table was a huge pile of tropical fruit that Wild Bill had peeled, cut and arranged on platters. There were pineapples, mangos, papayas, bananas, oranges, strawberries, and grapes. Looking at the array of fruit made their mouths water.

On another platter, there were four-dozen jumbo rock shrimp Wild Bill had arranged on ice with lemons and a bowl of his own cocktail sauce recipe.

"Protein," he said. "You need protein."

There was a whole wheel of Brie he had melted perfectly in the oven and surrounded on the table with baskets of freshly baked bread. They sat down around the table, smoked another bowl, cracked open bottles of Pacifica beer, and stared at the meal with wide eyes as they thought about the work ahead.

"Where do we start?" Krantz giggled.

"Just dig in," Wild Bill said, popping a shrimp into his mouth. Their eating quickly took on a rhythm in which they didn't speak to each other in words but communicated with grunts and groans of pleasure mixed with laughter. Each of them in turn was overwhelmed by the beauty of the moment Wild Bill had created. Time disappeared for a while and suddenly all the food was gone.

They sat back in disbelief, patted their stomachs, cleared the plates, and returned to the table for dessert. Wild Bill placed wafers at the bottom of each bowl and covered them with yogurt and two fistfuls of fresh plump blueberries. They ate every bite and when they were finished, they moved to the couches to rest ahead of whatever was next.

As the sun set outside, Wild Bill poured the vial of powdered mushrooms onto the glass table and divided it into four equal piles. They each swallowed their dose and sat waiting for the shrooms to kick in.

Wild Bill suggested that they head out to a club to dance and help their digestion along. Once there, they all felt slow and woozy on the dance floor. One second Jack felt drunk, the next he felt stoned, then tired and full from the food, and then, after juggling these sensations for a while, he sensed that he was beginning to shroom.

After fifteen minutes of the four of them awkwardly dancing, it became apparent that the club had little to offer them. They left and took a cab back to Krantz's place, where he lit a candle, plugged in the string of Christmas lights hanging on the wall, and put on William Orbit's *Strange Cargo III*.

"Water From A Vine Leaf" played through the speakers. Jack lay down on Krantz's couch and closed his eyes. Krantz, Wild Bill, and Virginia lay on the rug in the center of the floor in the shape of a triangle, each of their heads at one another's feet.

Jack fell into a deep mushroom trance and watched as an alien grid of patterns moved before his eyes, tubules of iridescent fluorescence, antifreeze greens and hot pinks; veins, levels, and layers of fluids pulsing, moving in all directions, each filled with meaning, the primal futuristic words of which were just out of reach of his mind's understanding.

Twenty minutes later the visions subsided and, as if by cue, all four of them simultaneously opened their eyes, stretched, looked at each other and laughed. They talked about what they had seen. Each of them had the same mushroom vision. The feast had come to a happy end. The next day, Wild Bill was gone, on to the film's next location.

A few years later, Jack watched the documentary about the making of *Natural Born Killers* that came with the director's cut of the film. In one scene, he caught a glimpse of Wild Bill standing in the background.

He was leaning against a wall next to some lighting, his arms crossed over his chest, watching as Oliver Stone gestured wildly to the actors as they worked out how to film the scene. He looked amused.

NUMBER 10 TO NOWHERE

Jack was in a funk about how things had been going since he arrived in Seattle. The dribble of temp agency jobs was not adding up to steady employment and consistent paychecks significant enough to allow him to afford his own apartment. His friends who had moved there ahead of him were involved with their already-established lives and invites to "welcome to the city" dinners and outings were no longer extended now that he had been there for a while.

His brother worked at Mario's in the Pike Place Market, so he could count on a bag or two of free produce, and after reading the want ads while sitting in front of the Westlake Center, he made the rounds of the food court's offerings of free samples to quell the rumblings of his hungry stomach.

For a few months after moving to Seattle, he qualified for unemployment benefits and once a week headed down to Belltown to drop off the required forms and pick up his check. Because he hadn't worked consistently the previous year, the checks were small and the benefits soon ran out.

His friend Amy had taken him in with the understanding that he would pay half the rent for her remarkably small studio a few blocks off 15th. It was his first taste of stability in a long time and he would feel eternally grateful for her gesture that allowed him some peace of mind while attempting to cobble together a new life.

The situation wasn't without its pitfalls, though. The size of the apartment meant that there was nowhere for either of them to go if they needed a bit of solitude. The love seat cushions on the floor were comfortable enough, but they were just that, love seat cushions on the floor. Then there were the nights when Amy's boyfriend came over for dinner, which made Jack feel like a heel despite the fact that neither of them had any problem with him being there.

Their life in the tiny apartment was mostly blissful, though. Jack went out of his way to be a good roommate by doing the dishes, going for walks to give Amy a bit of space now and then, and making sure he contributed towards the rent as promised even if it meant he'd have little money of his own.

Jack watched the news every night and kept her up to date about the day's developments in Bosnia and the siege of Sarajevo, though after a long day at work she usually was more in the mood for comedy or *Beverly Hills, 90210*. Jack didn't care for the show, but after a few weeks of watching it in silent disgust so as not to ruin Amy's enjoyment, he found he had developed TV star crushes on Brenda and Kelly and that he didn't care for Steve. Amy didn't like him either.

Some nights Jack returned to the apartment after a day spent wandering around town reading the want ads or working a temp agency shift to find that she had made dinner or picked up a to go order of Spicy Noodle from Jamjuree down the street. Some nights the bong made an appearance on the coffee table, almost always on Thursdays when *Friends*, *Seinfeld*, and *ER* were on.

Sometimes she picked up a movie from On 15th Video for them to watch and sometimes she suggested they head downtown to the Cinema UA 150 to see a $1.50 screening of a second run Hollywood blockbuster like *Speed* with Keanu Reeves, Sandra Bullock, and Dennis Hopper. On these occasions, Amy treated Jack to his ticket and he reciprocated by paying for the popcorn and soda from his small reserve of pocket money.

For a while, she got him some shifts cleaning offices at night, her second job in addition to her 9 to 5 day job at a local law firm. These shifts were irregular and while the influx of cash was welcome, it was disheartening to see so much evidence of people living established, steady lives on the desks he dusted. Pictures of happy families, trips abroad, and gatherings with friends seemed to adorn every desk, reminding Jack of his unsettled life.

The assignments the temp agency offered him were demeaning at worst, absurd at best. His first taste of employment in Seattle lasted just two days. He was sent to the bottling warehouse of a company that made flavored syrups to be added to coffee. His job was to stand on the line and place a cellophane topper onto the bottle cap before the bottles moved into the machine that sealed them tight.

The line foreman was an old grey-haired gentlemen somewhere in his sixties with a thick New York accent, a severe limp caused by an injury at a factory a long time ago, and a taste for telling raunchy jokes and bossing his employees around as if they were in the military and he was a commanding officer leading them on an important mission.

When Jack first showed up and introduced himself to the foreman, the man didn't look him in the eye and acted as if his presence was an imposition. He pointed to the line and told Jack to take his place next to the bottle capper.

"Firing up, boys!" he yelled when he switched on the line in the morning and after lunch breaks. The bottles rattled and started moving down the conveyors.

The line moved fast so there was little room for error, and if one fell behind, they had to press the red STOP button and draw everyone's attention to whoever screwed up.

Luckily Jack never had to hit the button, but after listening to the bottle capper's complaints about how he was getting paid less than the other employees on the line, Jack advised him to talk to the company owner and told him that he had every right to equal pay. The bottle capper fell silent and appeared to be deep in thought, during which time he started missing every other bottle.

He seemed oblivious to what was happening, so Jack leaned over and said, "Dude." The guy appeared to be startled to see that he had missed putting caps on so many bottles and hit the red button that brought the line to a stop. The foreman limped over to find out what was going on. The bottle capper shrugged and looked dejected.

"Stay focused!" the foreman shouted as he placed bottle caps on the bottles that had been missed before firing up the line again. The bottle capper told Jack that they had better not talk anymore because he didn't want to get in trouble. The rest of the day passed in a blur of syrup bottles passing by. It felt like a game more than a job. A dull game.

The next day when Jack showed up in the morning for work, the foreman was standing on the loading dock with the whole crew gathered around him and was clearly talking about Jack. Jack stood off to the side and listened as the old many explained to them that he didn't like him, didn't like the way he worked, and that if he had any say in the matter, today would be his last day.

Jack shook his head at the absurdity of it all and felt relieved when, during lunch break, the foreman came over to tell him he could go home because they only needed him for half the day. "Good riddance," Jack thought, as he left the warehouse behind. Some ways of making money were more work than the money was worth.

His next temp assignment sounded easy, a simple collating assignment. A company needed a dozen temps to come in and collate reports for a presentation the following day. After he arrived, he and the eleven other temps were taken to a conference room with no windows. Before them on the table were stacks and stacks of papers, folders, and binders. Some reports needed to be assembled in folders, others in binders. Some had to be bound by clips, others stapled.

The office manager explained what needed to be done and asked if there were any questions. Nobody said a word and he closed the door behind him; nobody said a word after the door was closed. Attempts to make small talk were rebuffed with disgusted silence. No one in the room wanted to be in the room. It was employment purgatory.

Compared to the bottling line, Jack didn't think it was such a bad assignment. He enjoyed the Zen-like repetition of collating, but by the end of the day, eight hours of miserable silence and faces made his body feel like he had performed eight hours of physical labor.

The next time Jack called the agency to see if there was work, they told him to show up at an office downtown the following day. It would probably be a long-term clerical assignment, they said, that might turn into a permanent position. Jack felt hopeful. Perhaps his luck was about to take a turn in the right direction.

When he showed up at the office on Monday morning, the secretary who was going to train him told him she was slammed and needed to take care of some things before she could get to him. She pointed to a desk and told him to wait there.

Jack sat and watched as she made phone calls, disappeared into offices with folders, and stopped to make office small talk and joke around with some of the other staff. An hour passed like this, then two, then three, and suddenly it was time for lunch. Jack asked how long he had for his break and said he planned to get a sandwich down the street.

The secretary explained that he needed to stay in the office for their monthly staff meeting and that lunch would be provided. She walked Jack into the employee lounge where rows of box lunches had been set up. Everyone from the top all the way down to Jack was in the room.

The boss thanked everyone for coming, said he was looking forward to hearing from everyone and that he hoped they could all generate some really positive energy to apply to the coming month. Before they ate, he asked that everyone in the room introduce themselves and explain something they were really excited about that the company was doing. Jack sunk into his seat and thought, "what the…?"

After each person spoke, the others clapped in unison and chanted that person's name. Jack wondered if he had stumbled into some kind of corporate cult. When it was his turn to speak, he said his name, explained that this was his first day, and that he looked forward to getting to know everybody. The boss looked at him and waited to hear what he was excited about, but the only thing that came to mind was, "I'm excited about lunch!"

Everyone laughed, clapped, and chanted his name. Jack really wanted to say that he was excited to get the hell out of there. After lunch, the secretary again explained that she had a lot of things to take care of before she could train him, but promised she would get to him soon. He continued to sit at his desk for the rest of the afternoon, doing nothing except smiling at the employees who passed by who said hello now that they knew his name.

The next two days passed in similar fashion, minus the office-wide lunches, which left him free to wander around downtown for an hour between the morning and afternoon sessions of wondering when he was going to do some work.

Maybe the assignment would go on forever like this, he thought. Maybe sitting there *was* the job. It was easy money, but doing nothing made time seem like it had slowed to a stop. He was relieved and disgusted when the agency called him early the next morning to tell him the company wouldn't need him after all. No explanation was given and that was that.

Jack was relieved because he didn't think he could have taken another day sitting at the desk. He was disgusted because it seemed like the city didn't want him to find his way. Each time he thought he was building up some momentum, things ground to a halt.

Instead of reading the want ads and making calls, Jack decided to do whatever he felt like doing with his day. He went back to sleep for a few hours and ate a late and lazy breakfast when he finally woke up close to what would have been lunch hour in the office. He looked out the window. It was a nice day, a good day to go exploring.

Standing on 15th a while later trying to figure out where he wanted to go, he saw the number 10 bus headed his way. He had taken it from 15th to downtown and back but had never ridden it past the stop in front of the supermarket. He decided to get on the bus and ride it as far as it went to explore that part of Capitol Hill and whatever was beyond.

Despite being broke, unemployed, and feeling generally downtrodden, Jack allowed himself to feel free and at ease. As the bus pulled away from the stop, Jack leaned against the window and settled in for what he expected to be an afternoon of adventure.

Just a few stops later, though, in front of the Lake View Cemetery, the bus turned right, went a little ways down a hill, and turned around again to head back in the direction from which they had just come.

"Bus ride to nowhere," Jack thought as he got off across the street from where he had gotten on. Only fifteen minutes had passed since the beginning of his "adventure." He sighed and returned in defeat to the apartment, where he sat and stared into space.

"The world isn't going anywhere," Jack thought, "and neither am I."

SNOW

Six months after arriving in Seattle, Jack Waste took the bus from Capitol Hill to the University of Washington to do some literary research. Light flurries were falling as he entered the library. Several hours later, Jack looked up from his books, saw that it was dark outside, and decided it was time to head back to the apartment. He returned his books to their shelves and set out into the evening.

The snow had accumulated what looked like an eighth of an inch on the ground. Jack kicked at it with his feet as he waited for the bus. A pretty woman with blonde hair crossed the street and joined him. She asked if he had seen the number 43 go by. No, he told her, he was waiting for it too, adding that in no other city he had lived would a bus be late because of so little snow, to which she replied that she had just moved there too and couldn't believe it either.

A stranger walked by and interrupted their small talk to announce that because of the snow, buses had been stranded and would not be able to make it up the hill. Jack asked if he had heard an official announcement to that effect. No, the man said, but he had seen several buses pulled over by the side of the road.

Jack looked up the street from which the bus would arrive but did not see any reason for it to be unable to navigate it and thought the man was being overdramatic in his assessment of the situation. There was barely any snow on the ground. The man trudged off down the street and the woman told Jack that she was going to start walking.

"I'm going to wait a few more minutes," he said, "I'm sure the bus will show up." She looked at him for a moment, said "okay" and walked off into the falling snow.

Ten minutes later, Jack found himself to be the only person who still believed the bus was coming. All the others who had been waiting at the stop had disappeared into the night. The snowfall was increasing and now there was more than a quarter inch on the ground.

He looked down at the woman's footprints in the snow, sighed, and set out to walk to the next stop. Maybe by then the bus would come, he thought, but when he got to the next stop and looked behind him, there was no bus coming and he resigned himself to walking back to Capitol Hill.

Jack followed her tracks to the other side of the cut and the 520 bridge and off ramp, where they branched off to the right into a neighborhood he was unfamiliar with. His path home was to the left and up the hill. He thought about how she had hesitated for a moment before walking away from the bus stop and realized that he had probably let a spark of connection slip through his fingers. He resigned himself to his fate and proceeded up the hill.

A young man and woman ran past him laughing. The woman slid to a halt in the sidewalk snow, turned with fists clenched towards the sky as if in victory, and yelled, "It's SNOWING!!!"

She turned and continued running with her friend up a side street, at the top of which Jack saw people with flattened cardboard boxes making ready to sled down.

"Yeah," he thought, "it's snowing all right. What's the big deal?" It was a long, dreary march and his feet were sore and soaking wet, but he finally found himself inside the apartment, where he dropped his backpack and sat down exhausted on the couch. Amy had left a note that said she was staying at her boyfriend's for the night. Jack had the place to himself. He turned off the lights and went to bed.

As he lay there, he pictured the woman's footsteps disappearing as they were covered over with new falling snow. He wondered what she was doing and pondered what his night and the tomorrows that followed might have been like if he had chosen to walk with her instead of waiting like a fool for the bus that never arrived.

A few years later, Jack understood what a rare occurrence snow falling in Seattle really was, as was the appearance of strangers at bus stops who weren't really strangers.

THE ROLLING STONES

Jack Waste sat on the couch and watched the start of the 10 o'clock news. He and Amy had eaten dinner earlier and watched some television and now she was getting ready to go to bed. The big story at the top of the newscast was that The Rolling Stones were in town and about to play their show at the Kingdome. The news cut to a live shot from inside the stadium, where a reporter on the scene explained that the opening band was playing and that The Rolling Stones were due to take the stage in thirty minutes.

Jack was just about ready to call it a night too, but instead announced, "I'm going to see The Rolling Stones."

"Okay," Amy said, laughing, "have fun."

Jack stood up, put on his jacket, left the apartment, and walked down the street. He walked slowly but with purpose, taking in every detail of his new neighborhood. He walked from Republican to John, where he turned and walked down to Broadway, then over to Pine and down towards downtown. He turned down 5th and walked for a while, continuing to take in the sights of the city in a relaxed fashion. He cut down to 2nd Ave. and saw the Kingdome on the near horizon.

A few blocks away, he began to see scalpers offering tickets. Jack had little money in his pocket and could not afford the prices they were asking, and anyway, he had a different plan in mind: he was going to Jedi his way in.

Once he was within a hundred yards of one of the gates, he decided he was going to walk calmly forward as if he already had a ticket in hand.

A hundred feet away, Jack's heart started to beat a little faster as he anticipated the moment's arrival, and then, just fifty feet from the entrance when he was about to start doubting his plan, a man announced loudly without turning around, "I have one ticket for five dollars, I'm not stopping, who wants it?"

Jack ran ahead and handed the man a crumpled five-dollar bill. Just as he was about to pass through the gate, the man handed Jack the ticket. Jack followed him inside, both of them laughing about the transaction.

The ticket was for a nosebleed seat on the third level. Jack continued walking up the spiral ramp and, upon reaching the top, a group of people smoking a joint turned and offered it to him. He laughed at how perfectly everything had fallen into place, pinched the joint in his fingertips, and took a big hit.

"Finish it," one of the revelers said. Jack Waste did just that.

He walked to his aisle and looked down at the ticket. His seat was in the front row. The crowd roared in welcome as The Stones appeared on stage and started playing "Not Fade Away." Jack stepped down the stairs towards his row and, realizing how high up he was, felt a wave of vertigo kick in. He tripped while stepping down the last step, just enough so that he had to steady himself on the rail to keep from falling over. It was a long way down.

What had be been thinking? He didn't like heights and would not have been able to sit the entire show in that front row seat without panicking. He turned and bounded up the stairs and leaned against the wall of the entry passageway as The Stones played "Undercover of the Night."

Jack realized he had almost died. He stood there trembling for a few minutes before he calmed down enough to return to the present moment. An excited fan grabbed Jack's arm and yelled into his ear, "It's the Rolling Stones! It's the Rolling Stones!"

The rest of the show passed in a blur of rock and roll euphoria. "I'm a monkey!" Jack screamed with the crowd.

FOCUS GROUP

When Jack first moved to Seattle and was broke and looking for work, his brother told him about the Gilmore Research Group and how you could get your name on a list to participate in product focus groups and make fifty bucks for an hour of your time.

Jack called them and told them he wanted to be put on their list. They took his name and phone number and said they would be in touch. A few weeks later they called and asked him to participate in a focus group on computer games. Jack had never played a game on his computer but said that he had so he could get into the study. A few nights later, he made fifty bucks for sitting around a table with seven other men talking about the packaging on a bunch of computer games handed out for them to examine.

"Easy money," Jack thought.

Jack was taking a nap when Gilmore Research called again some months later. He tried to wake himself up to be ready for the questions they would ask. If you gave one wrong answer you would be excluded from the study and your chance for an easy fifty bucks would go down the drain.

"How many times have you eaten at a fast food restaurant in the past month?" the group organizer asked.

"Oh, I'd say about ten times," Jack said, not sure if he'd eaten fast food even once in that time, though he'd certainly walked by Jack In The Box and Taco Bell on Broadway several times a week.

"Good," the organizer said, and Jack knew he was on the right track. "Please list the franchises you have visited."

"Burger King, Jack In The Box, McDonald's, and Taco Bell," Jack answered.

She told him that he had qualified for a focus group study taking place the following Thursday night. He would be paid fifty dollars for an hour of his time spent talking about a fast food-related topic.

"Sounds good," Jack said, wrote down the time and date on a piece of paper, hung up the phone, and returned to his nap. A week later, he hopped on the bus and headed down to the Gilmore Research office on Eastlake.

He went to a nearby cafe beforehand and ate a delicious turkey breast sandwich with cranberry sauce and a pickle. He read *The Stranger* and *The Seattle Weekly* until it was time to go to the study.

At the reception desk, he was given a name card to put in front of him on the table and told to enjoy some "refreshments." The "refreshments" were pretzels, M & M's, and soda. Jack leafed through a magazine and looked at the seven other guys and wondered if they were really fast food eaters or if they had embellished their answers too. When it was time to go in, a man came out of the study room, looked at them, put eye drops in his eyes, clapped his hands and said, "Okay, let's do this thing!"

Inside the conference room, he asked them to place their name cards in front of them and pointed to the wall length mirror behind him. Behind the one-way mirror, he explained, were representatives from the company doing the study. He asked the study group to wave hello to them. Jack didn't raise his hand to wave like the other guys.

"They're probably in there making faces at us," Jack thought.

The focus group leader announced that the company they would be talking about that night was Jack In The Box. "Yes!" one of the other guys said, pumping his fist in front of him. He seemed really into it.

For the next hour, they were shown Jack In The Box commercials and asked to rate them and the product being advertised. They were also asked to discuss their thoughts about the ads, the ideas they were trying to convey and how effective they were in doing so.

Jack had seen all the ads before: Jack In The Box ball head on a talk show, Jack and his ball-headed son throwing a baseball to each other, a new employee at Jack In The Box being fired for suggesting to Jack that he should raise the price of his ninety-nine cent menu items.

The focus group leader was a strange and funny man. He was very hyper and kept trying to pump the group up to get them excited about what they were talking about and to talk louder so the mikes could hear what they were saying.

The other five guys were pretty funny too. They all seemed to get really into the study right from the start and all seemed to be true fast food connoisseurs.

One guy spoke about how he always "got burned" when he tried one of the new products that Jack In The Box offered instead of sticking with his tried and true double cheeseburger.

Another guy spoke about how he always ordered his burgers or sandwiches minus something they normally came with so they would have to make him a fresh one on the spot.

After each commercial, they were asked, on a scale of 1 to 5, how inclined they would be to go to Jack In The Box based on their viewing of the commercials. Some said they would definitely try the product based on criteria such as how fresh the lettuce looked, how red the tomatoes were, or how cheap the price was.

Jack rated each commercial a 1. When asked why, he said he would not be inclined to go to Jack In The Box after watching the commercials because the actual experience of going to Jack In The Box was never like the commercials. He described in detail the homeless people, junkies, drunks, and lunatics that frequented his neighborhood Jack In The Box, how the employees always appeared to be stressed, unhappy, and overworked, and how the food never looked like it did in the ads.

Jack said that he would be more inclined to eat at Jack In The Box if they filmed a commercial there on a Friday night that depicted its reality. The guy two seats away from Jack began to laugh hysterically and covered his mouth as he shook uncontrollably.

"Dude," he said, "SO true." The moderator quickly called on someone else.

Jack noticed that the focus group leader touched his ear a lot and when he turned his head he saw what looked like a hearing aid the color of his skin. Whenever he touched his ear, he would ask a question after, so Jack figured they were feeding him lines from behind the mirror.

Jack decided to see if he could make the guy two seats down laugh again the next time it was his turn to talk. When the moderator went around the table and asked when they were most inclined to eat at Jack In The Box, breakfast, lunch, or dinner, Jack said late at night after last call when everyone had left the bars and was so loaded that it made sense to eat there. Again, the guy broke out in a spasm of uncontrollable laughter, and again, the moderator quickly moved on to someone else. They didn't seem to want to hear the truth.

The guy seated across from Jack said he didn't go to Jack In The Box expecting the chicken sandwich to look as thick, fresh, and juicy as it did on television.

Another guy described the wilted lettuce, oozy tomato, and sliver of overcooked meat he expected to get when he ate there. The moderator moved on to another question.

The group was asked to comment on how the ball head Jack character came off to in the ads. Did they like him? Did they like him better in the old ads?

A guy sitting across from Jack said that he didn't care for the new Jack, but preferred the old, more sarcastic Jack from past commercials. He said he hoped they would get back to depicting him in that light again in the future.

Finally, the hour was up just when Jack was beginning to enjoy the experience. The moderator told them he had a special surprise and picked up a box from the floor. It was filled with Jack In The Box car antenna ball heads.

Jack laughed happily with the rest of the guys, as some small part of him always wanted one of those when he saw them on TV even though he didn't have a car.

The moderator thanked the group for their participation and directed them to the front desk to receive their payment. At the front desk, they were each given an envelope with a crisp fifty-dollar bill inside.

On the elevator, as soon as the doors closed, he and the other guys looked at each other and busted out laughing.

"That was surreal," the guy who had laughed at Jack's comments said.

Outside, still laughing, they all went their separate ways. Jack got on the bus, hoping to run into a friend when he got back to the hill so he could spread some of his wealth around at Ileen's, The Comet, The Easy, or Moe's.

"Funny money," he thought, rubbing the fifty-dollar bill between his fingers. He felt alive and ready for the rest of the night.

THE RICHEST PEOPLE IN THE WORLD

Circa 1994 after moving to Seattle, Jack worked a series of odd jobs that didn't add up to steady employment nor make him feel like he really lived in the city.

He slept on his friend Amy's couch cushions on the floor of her small studio apartment, and though he was able to pay his share of the rent, there wasn't enough money coming in for him to be able to set any aside towards an apartment of his own.

One afternoon between paychecks, he walked down Broadway wishing he had enough money to take himself out to lunch. While waiting for the light to change at the corner of Broadway & Thomas, he counted his money for the second time that day, but the amount was still the same: three dollars and forty-eight cents in random change.

The light changed and Jack crossed the street. Sitting at a window table with a lady friend inside Angel's Thai Food was Paul Allen, one of the richest people in the world. They weren't talking when Jack passed, just staring out the window watching the passersby, all of whom seemed to be oblivious to Allen's identity.

Jack clenched the money he had in his hand and laughed to himself about being so broke as he walked by one of the richest people in the world.

Circa 1995-97, Jack Waste worked as a banquet waiter at The Camlin Hotel, where he was the sole waiter for Blue Oyster Cult's private dinner before their concert, for which they tipped him fifty dollars. He also worked at the Washington State Convention Center, The Sheraton Hotel, and The Warwick Hotel.

After living on the couch for a year and feeling like he would never have his own place again, Jack saved enough money to move into a studio apartment on Capitol Hill after just a month of waiting tables.

He felt like he was back on his feet after the long slow fade that seemed to have happened quite suddenly after the luxury of grad school came to an end.

Jack had read F. Scott Fitzgerald's "The Crack-Up" and was ready in a literary way for a downturn of circumstances, but as one witnesses their decline for real when life takes a detour in the wrong direction, it all seems to be happening to someone else even though that someone else is you.

He finally had an apartment, steady work, and a girlfriend. Life felt the way he thought life was supposed to feel after paying his dues for a year and a half after moving to Seattle, except that despite finally regularizing his existence, a waiter is only as rich as the number of shifts he or she can handle. If they're smart, they wear a back brace and dig in for the long haul and salt money away for the day when the body gives out instead of frittering it away on after shift drinks with their fellow waiters.

Jack was a pretty good waiter once he learned the ropes and took some pride in doing a good job, but once he realized there wasn't much more to the job beyond what he learned to become a good waiter, he focused on learning how to be a bad waiter without any of the customers or managers noticing. The work got easier and the tips stayed the same after he figured out a variety of shortcuts that should have been obvious from the start. For example, he discovered that instead of refilling his table's water glasses, the guests were content to refill their own if he set a fresh pitcher down in the center of the table and walked away.

Jack loved the easy camaraderie that developed after working just one shift with his fellow waiters, telling each other stories and joking around in the midst of the flurry of service, and again afterwards, pumped with post-shift adrenaline, sharing stories over the employee meal and making plans to spill out to some bar where more stories were told over beers. He loved the stories, the characters, the back hall swearing, talking to the chefs about their work, and the flow of the night when the waiters appeared to be performing a choreographed dance.

Then the next day arrived and he was scheduled for an early morning breakfast shift after working a double the day before and he didn't know if his body and mind could take it until he got up and running and into the flow, and on it went from shift to shift. The money was good. Waiting tables was truly labor, but at the end of the night when he calculated his pay, the money was so good it sometimes almost seemed like he had gotten away with something he shouldn't have.

It helped that Seattle was really happening then with the dot-com explosion and lots of money being thrown around to put on extravagant events. There were plenty of shifts and hours for any waiter who wanted them. The week Microsoft rented out the whole Sheraton Hotel, there were so many events scheduled that Jack was able to work seventy hours.

One moment, he was in the Grand Ballroom pouring coffee and listening to Bill Gates explain the future of the world, the next he was eating the same entrée for his employee shift meal that Bill Gates ate during the banquet. Jack liked getting paid to be a part of whatever event was going on that those in attendance had to pay for. Weddings, reunions, sports awards, auctions, Oscar night galas, wine and food tastings—whatever the occasion, Jack had a backstage pass and a part to play in the entertainment.

After a year of working at the Sheraton, word went around that Bill Gates senior was going to get married at Bill Gates Jr.'s estate in the finishing stages of construction on Lake Washington, and that a selection of the hotel's waiters would soon be made to work the night. Two weeks later, Jack and the other waiters who found their name on the list were told when and where to meet in front of the hotel, from where they would be driven in the hotel van out to the Gates estate.

It was a very hot summer day, the kind one dreads having to go to work. Jack walked down to the hotel and stood joking around with the rest of the waiters before piling into the van. A little while later, somewhere on the other side of Lake Washington, the hotel van driver pulled into a parking lot some distance from the Gates estate, where they were told, for security reasons, to get into a second set of vans owned or rented by Bill Gates himself. The drivers of these vans wore earpieces and had bulges beneath their jackets that suggested they were armed.

Later, at the estate, they would see numerous other gentlemen with bulges beneath their suit jackets, and once in passing, when one of these gentleman leaned over to pick something up, Jack caught a glimpse of a holster and what looked like an Uzi.

After they arrived, they were given a tour of the areas where they would serve a reception and later the dinner. They set the tables, filled the pitchers with ice water, and laid out the *mise en place*, then were told it was time to take their break and eat their employee meal of box lunches with sandwiches, pickles, and chips.

Since there was no employee break room, they were told to sit and eat on Bill Gates's private pier. As box lunches went, Jack thought, it was a pretty good one.

He said to his fellow waiters, "look at us, we're royalty!"

Tour boats passed by every so often and lingered a few hundred feet from the shore. Jack and the rest of the waiters waved as the people on board raised their cameras to take pictures. After they finished eating, they were told that they were free to walk around the still unfinished estate before the party started so as to familiarize themselves with the areas they would be serving the guests.

Jack and a couple other waiters wandered from skeleton room to skeleton room, stopping along the way to take in the Gates library, complete with skylight and indoor fountain.

Nowhere in the house was livable yet or even fully recognizable, and it was only through reading the notecards taped to the walls that they were able to identify what each future room was going to be.

After this idyllic break it was time to get to work. The guests were beginning to arrive by boat following the wedding ceremony that had taken place elsewhere in the city. Jack was put on beverage duty in an area outside next to the roofed-over pool that had a hundred underwater speakers for piped-in music.

The sunlight on the lake was beautiful when the event began and sent shimmering gem-like ripples of light dancing across the proceedings. It was in this light that Jack came face to face with one of the world's richest people. He stood at the ready holding a silver tray, upon which were two types of water in wine glasses, regular and sparking, hoping it would not slip through his white-gloved hands.

Bill Gates walked towards Jack and, without looking him in the eye, pointed at the glasses and asked, "Regular water?"

Jack nodded to the side of the tray that held the regular water and Gates took a glass and cocktail napkin and returned to a group of guests on the grass next to the lake. Jack made a mental note that there had been no "thank you" or acknowledgment of his service.

The rest of the night unfolded as a series of surreal moments as they witnessed the behind the scenes reality of the significantly wealthy.

Entertainer Dick Martin was escorted past the waiters and into the dining room to sing to the guests, his entourage announcing, to move the waiters out of their way, "talent coming through, talent coming through!"

The waiters used the line for the rest of the night and at the hotel for months after. It never got old.

After dinner, they stood on the grass near the shore with the rest of the guests and watched Bill Gates Sr. wave goodbye before climbing into a helicopter that lifted up and flew off into the night sky towards the Seattle skyline.

Once Jack and the rest of the waiters were transferred back into the hotel van and felt free to speak, they all laughed at the unreality of the whole evening and told stories about their experiences.

Soon after, they found themselves drinking three-dollar beers amongst the regulars at a bar up the street from the hotel, shouting "talent coming through, talent coming through," while on the other side of the lake, the pier where they had eaten their box lunches bobbed in the night.

Circa 1995, a few months after starting work at The Sheraton, meeting his girlfriend, and moving into his own apartment, they went to Angel's Thai Food for lunch.

As they sat and stared out at the passersby, Jack realized that he was sitting at the exact table and in the exact chair where Paul Allen sat a year earlier when Jack was nearly broke.

He hadn't increased his net worth much since that day, but sitting there with his girlfriend watching his past self walk by and look in the window, he at least felt like one of the richest people in the world, and though they were only drinking water, he raised a toast to the occasion and clinked his girlfriend's glass as the passersby walked by oblivious to who he was.

PRESIDENT OF THE CZECH REPUBLIC

Jack was working a lunch banquet one day on the main floor of the Sheraton Hotel when he was sent up to the thirty-fifth to help clean up.

On the way up the elevator, another waiter told him that it was a business luncheon to create opportunities between the United States and Eastern Europe and that the President of the Czech Republic was the special guest of honor.

Jack had Czech and Slovak heritage from his father's side of the family and looked forward to hearing what the President had to say. He listened from the back of the room as he answered questions from the audience.

When it was over, Jack stood in the hallway where the President was going to pass on his way to the elevator with his small security detail.

Jack planned to say hello, but when he came through the door, the President had a stern look on his face, stared straight ahead, and did not say hello to any of the waiters.

Disappointed, Jack went into the banquet room to help clean up. He noticed that the President had not eaten his dessert, a blueberry tart. He picked up a fork and ate it standing where the President had stood to give his speech and take questions from the audience.

The other waiters laughed when Jack spoke into the microphone to announce that he was eating the President of the Czech Republic's dessert.

When he was finished, he dropped the plate and fork into a bus tub and got back to work.

TERRY BRADSHAW

Pittsburgh Steelers quarterback Terry Bradshaw was the motivational speaker at a banquet luncheon one day tied in with the promotion of some new software.

The sponsors had decorated one half of the ballroom to look like a football stadium. From floor to ceiling on every side of the room was a mural of fans cheering at a sporting event that made you feel like you were in the middle of the football field with Terry when he was recounting his motivational football anecdotes.

People dressed in referee outfits handed out free software. Terry threw a couple of tiny footballs into the audience and everyone went crazy trying to catch one. After the motivational session, the guests moved to the other side of the ballroom for lunch.

Near the end, as Jack was waiting for everybody to leave so he could begin cleaning the room, he noticed Bradshaw get up from his seat and make for the door.

As he walked by, Jack stuck out his hand and said, "Hello, Mr. Bradshaw, how are you today?"

Terry reached out and shook Jack's hand without looking him in the eyes.

"Gotta run," he said, and disappeared through the door and into the hotel lobby beyond.

DICK CLARK

Many corporations held functions in the hotel's grand ballroom. This big room was Jack's workplace. Many of the banquets featured ornate set pieces and designs based on themes chosen by the companies who rented out the room for their events.

One night, Boeing held a banquet to celebrate the completion of one of its new airplanes. The whole ballroom was decked out in black curtains and gold trim in a look paying homage to the forties and fifties. Jack was chatting with another waiter a few minutes before the banquet was scheduled to begin. One of the doors opened and a man on crutches hobbled in. It was Dick Clark.

"Dude," Jack said, "here comes Dick Clark."

"Yeah, right," the other waiter said, thinking Jack was messing with him, but then, as Dick Clark came closer, he leaned over and said, "Dude, that *is* Dick Clark!"

As Dick Clark limped past, Jack said, "Good evening, Mr. Clark, what did you do to your knee?"

"Ankle," he corrected Jack gruffly, then added, also gruffly, "skiing."

The other waiter looked at Jack and they both laughed. Dick Clark, one of the nicest personalities on television, had just been totally gruff with them.

When he was introduced to the full ballroom later in the evening, though, he bounded onto the stage with a big smile on his face and without the crutches and gave a speech about how exciting the new year was going to be for Boeing and how excited he was to be a part of the celebration.

At the end of his comments, he directed everyone's attention to a curtain that stretched from one side of the ballroom to the other. With a wide sweep of his hand, he introduced the band for the night. The curtain opened and everyone clapped and cheered as the other half of the ballroom was revealed and a fifties cover band kicked into its first song. People stood up and made for the dance floor like lemmings as Jack poured wine.

For the rest of the night, every time he and the other waiter crossed paths, they replayed a variation of the exchange they'd had with Dick Clark.

"Ankle," one of them said gruffly.

"Skiing," the other said in response, also gruffly. The skit didn't grow old for a long time.

HILLARY CLINTON'S SALSA

Jack worked a luncheon banquet at which First Lady Hillary Clinton was going to be the guest speaker. The Secret Service had arrived the day before to scope things out and on the day of the event they did a sweep of the Grand Ballroom to look for bombs under all the tables while Jack and the rest of the waiters were setting things up.

None of the waiters would see the First Lady, though, as she was going to enter the room after they had served lunch to all of the guests.

On instructions from the Secret Service, they were told that after they set down the desserts, they would have to leave the room and head straight to the employee cafeteria until the speech was over and Clinton had left the hotel.

As Jack waited for the elevator to go down to cafeteria level, he heard a big round of applause. The First Lady had entered the ballroom. Later, when they were called back up to clear the ballroom, he passed through the room she had used as her pre-event area.

The hotel had set up a few couches, a table, some phones, and chips and salsa. Jack found a piece of paper with a list of names on it. It looked like notes the First Lady had written about the people who were going to receive special awards at the banquet. Next to every name there were a few details about each.

Jack took a chip from the bowl and dipped it into the First Lady's salsa. He stood there for a minute and ate a few more of the First Lady's chips before heading into the ballroom to help with the cleanup.

BILL CLINTON'S HAND

President Bill Clinton was in town to give a campaign speech at the Pike Place Market. A few weeks earlier, Jack saw an announcement in the paper explaining how to get a free ticket for admission into the event, but once the day arrived he wasn't sure if he felt like going.

He had to work a double shift at The Sheraton and it was raining. He wasn't sure he wanted to end a long day standing in the rain getting wet. As he sat with one of the other waiters eating his shift lunch when he was finished, though, Jack decided he probably wouldn't get the chance to see another President up close. He told the other waiter he was going to see the President.

"Okay," he said with an amused look in his eyes. "Tell him I said hello."

Jack set out from the hotel and walked towards the market. When he got there, he saw that all the side streets were packed with people and that the line to get in stretched from one end of the market to the other.

If he made it into the standing area his ticket allowed him access to, he saw that he would still be almost a football field away from the President. As he stood there deciding whether or not he wanted to stay, he noticed an official-looking person with a walkie-talkie leading a group of people towards what appeared to be a side access gate that bypassed the crowd.

Recognizing the opportunity, Jack made a split-second decision to join them and blended in behind the last person in the group. An usher smiled and said hello as he held the gate open for them to pass and Jack walked with the group almost the entire length of the market to a fenced-in standing area a block away from the stage, where the band Heart was singing acoustic versions of their songs as warm-up act to Clinton's speech.

"Not bad," Jack thought, "but maybe I can do better." He kept his eye on the passageway to the side of the crowd and noticed that people who looked like local dignitaries were being led past Jack's area towards still another fenced-in area right next to the stage. Once again, he waited for his moment and blended in behind the next group that passed and tried to project an attitude that said to the world he was exactly where he was supposed to be.

He saw that he would have to pass through a Secret Service checkpoint to make it through the final gate, but there was no turning back, and if he did, he would probably appear to be suspicious and that would make things worse. He gripped his folded ticket in his hand and prepared to act dumb if there was a problem.

The Secret Service agent asked him to put his keys and wallet in a plastic container and ran his metal detector wand up and down Jack's body, after which he said, "thank you, sir," and waved Jack in. Jack now found himself in what appeared to be the VIP area. He recognized a few city council members from having seen them in the paper and a couple times at various civic banquets at the hotel.

He looked back out over the crowd towards the far end of the market where he would have been standing had he not made his Jedi move.

After some time had passed without the President appearing, Jack's feet began to ache and, except for the part of his body covered by his waterproof jacket, he was getting wet from the steady drizzle. He decided to ask a woman standing at the entrance to the VIP area when Clinton was scheduled to arrive. She had a clipboard, a walkie-talkie, and an identification badge, so he figured she would probably know.

As soon as he began to speak, though, he recognized he had made a mistake. Instead of just blending in with the crowd, he had now drawn attention to himself.

The woman looked him up and down and asked, "Who are you?"

"I'm Jack Waste," Jack said with a smile, confidently repeating his question in an attempt to distract her from further inquiry.

"How did you get into this area?" she asked. Now Jack thought he was in trouble, but he remained confident and calm and pulled out the ticket from his pocket. His ticket was pink. He had noticed that some in the VIP area had blue tickets. The woman looked at his ticket, then at the Secret Service agent who had wanded Jack when he entered.

The Secret Service agent looked at Jack, recognized him from their interaction a half hour earlier, nodded and said, "he's good."

The woman folded Jack's ticket and, while handing it back to him, said, "The President will be here shortly."

Jack turned and blended back in with the VIP crowd. He sidled up to a gentleman waving an American flag and asked him if he was enjoying himself so as to appear, if the woman was still looking at him, that he knew someone and really did belong.

When he looked back, though, she was no longer paying attention to him or the VIP crowd, as the President's motorcade had just pulled up.

Jack took his camera out of his pocket and began taking pictures as Clinton emerged from his limousine. He waved at the crowd and shook the hands of the officials waiting for him before walking towards the stairs to the stage, which was enclosed in what appeared to be bulletproof glass. Jack noticed that men had appeared on the rooftops surrounding the market; more Secret Service or local law enforcement, he assumed.

The crowd roared as Clinton greeted them. It felt more like a rock concert than a political rally. Some in the crowd appeared to have tears in their eyes. Others clasped their hands, jumped up and down with excitement, and responded to everything Clinton said in similar fashion as he encouraged them to support his re-election bid.

At the end of the speech, he waved to the crowd as they continued to applaud and scream. Jack thought he would return to his limousine, but instead, Clinton walked down the steps on the opposite side of the stage and entered a passageway in front of the the VIP crowd. Jack had made his way to the front of this area during Clinton's speech to try to get a better angle of him speaking from the stage. Now Clinton was walking towards him and when he passed would be just a few feet away.

Both men and women in the VIP area surged forward and screamed Clinton's name. He smiled and reached his arms into the crowd. People grasped his hands and patted his arms as the Secret Service agents around him scanned the crowd for suspicious activity. Jack felt himself shoved from behind as someone tried to push through to get closer to the President, but Jack held his ground.

When Clinton was just three feet away, Jack reached out while raising his camera to try to take a picture of his hand touching the President's. He briefly gripped Clinton's hand before moved on and he got the shot. As he took the picture, Jack was laughing at the absurdity of the situation. Clinton briefly looked into Jack's eyes as he passed and then was whisked towards his waiting limousine, where he stopped and turned to wave once more to the crowd.

Everyone in the VIP area was gushing with excitement. Jack turned and moved down the side passageway back towards the other end of the market and was able to get ahead of everyone else in the crowd who had yet to start moving towards the exit.

He walked up Pike and joined the rush hour crowd of people getting off work and shoppers coming and going on their way from one store to another. He continued walking up towards Capitol Hill and returned to the apartment, where he lay down to take a nap.

The next day at the hotel, Jack told the other waiter that he had succeeded in meeting the President when they sat down together to eat their shift lunch. Jack had purchased a copy of the *Seattle Times* on the way to work that morning and now read about Clinton's visit. When he turned the page to read the rest of the story a few pages into the paper, Jack first looked at the accompanying photo.

Taken from the stage above and behind the President, the photo showed Clinton working the crowd of smiling faces, in the center of which was Jack's. The photographer had captured the exact moment Jack was laughing at the absurdity of the situation. He handed the paper to the other waiter and pointed at the picture. He ooked at it, smiled, and looked at Jack.

"Jack," he said, "you're famous!" They both laughed before returning to their lunch.

SONICS IN 7!

The 1995-96 Sonics were epic. Jack and his girlfriend rarely missed a game and watched them play at home or out at a bar where everyone was out to watch them too.

He preferred to watch at home, though, so he could hear announcer Kevin Calabro's play-by-play poetry and the signature catch phrases the team inspired.

The sound of falling rain outside and the Sonics on the television inside made for some powerful rhythm and jazz.

Jack occasionally ran into members of the team around town. One afternoon at Tower Records, Jack looked up from browsing the racks to see Shawn Kemp, the "Reign Man," browsing in the next aisle.

Kemp was at the height of his powers, a mythological figure the other browsers spoke of in hushed whispers as they basked in his presence.

While setting tables for a banquet at The Sheraton one afternoon, Jack looked up to see Detlef Schrempf walking towards him. He was there to participate in the evening's fundraising event. Jack was tempted to bellow Calabro's catch phrase he used whenever Schrempf made a spectacular play, "Achtung, Baby!" but simply said hello.

At the end of a banquet he worked at Key Arena set up on the floor of the arena where the Sonics played, Jack saw Gary Payton heading his way.

"Hello, Mr. Payton" Jack said.

"Hey, how you doing?" Payton said, and shook Jack's hand.

Afterwards, Jack told the other waiters he had felt the force of Payton's basketball powers in the grip of his hand.

One of them extended his hand and said, "let me see."

"I can feel it!" he exclaimed as he shook Jack's hand. All the waiters laughed before getting back to work clearing the dirty dishes.

Jack and his girlfriend watched Game 7 of the epic Western Conference Finals series against the Utah Jazz at Ileen's on Broadway. After the Sonics won and moved on to play for the championship against Michael Jordan and the Chicago Bulls, the city erupted in euphoria.

People cheered and waved at passing cars as they walked down the street and drivers honked their horns and yelled "Sonics!" out their windows.

There was palpable excitement in the air all around the city for the next week, and even though the Sonics returned from Chicago down two games to none and lost the first of three home games to put themselves in a 3-0 hole, the excitement didn't wane.

The Sonics won Game 4 to make the series 3-1 and it felt like they had rediscovered their swagger after initially appearing to be intimidated by Jordan and the Bulls.

The next night, Jack went to Linda's to have a beer with some friends. As they chatted, Jack noticed Dennis Rodman of the Bulls enter the bar with three other people. Rodman and his entourage sat at the table in the bar's upper level window. A low murmur ran through the room as everyone realized who was amongst them.

Rodman sat nursing a beer while draping his arm around a young woman by his side. Jack could hear people at other tables talking smack about Rodman and the Bulls, but not one voice was raised. It was a polite Seattle crowd.

Rodman and his crew left after they finished their drinks and walked up the street. Jack and his friends decided to call it a night a few minutes later. Jack felt like having one more beer before heading home, though, so he walked up Pine and over to Pike to go to The Comet for a schooner.

As he neared his old apartment building next to the gas station, Jack noticed Rodman sitting in the passenger seat of a car parked in front of Ballet Restaurant. The young woman and Rodman's other friend were in the back seat. The driver got into the car and started its engine. Rodman leaned his head back against the headrest and closed his eyes.

As the car pulled away, Jack yelled as loud as he could, "SONICS IN 7!!!"

Rodman opened his eyes and looked startled.

"Fuck you!" the guy in the back seat yelled. Jack watched as the car disappeared towards downtown.

The Sonics won the next game to make it 3-2 and extend the series to a sixth game back in Chicago. Jack was quite sure his decisive action had helped secure the victory.

THE HIGHLANDS

"I realized that the world does not represent a struggle at all, or a predaceous sequence of chance events, but shimmering bliss, beneficient trepidation, a gift bestowed on us and unappreciated."
Vladimir Nabokov, *Beneficence*

"I'm on my way over to pick you up," she said.

"Okay," Jack said. "I'm ready." He hung up the phone and put some things into his backpack. The first Washingtonian he had become friends with since moving to Seattle had invited him to a mansion party.

He didn't know what to expect. He felt like he was going on a trip. His bag packed with a change of clothes, he lay back on his bed and stared at the ceiling. He was tired from the past month's social events.

When the rainy season began, everyone hid out inside, held back by the rain, but after four or five weeks, restlessness and the need to commune with friends and strangers kicked in.

This was the official beginning of the party season, when crazy house parties were held beneath the ceiling of clouds, cold, and rain, and when the weather seemed to inspire wanton pagan euphoria.

He heard her car pull up outside. He grabbed his backpack and walked out into the night. The air was cool. The sky was clear with big billowy clouds moving through. The moon was a sliver and the Space Needle shimmered like a jewel.

He climbed into her '66 Dodge Dart and buckled his seat belt. They pulled away from the curb. At the entrance to the highway, she put *Led Zeppelin III* into the player and cranked the volume. "Immigrant Song" kicked in as they drove north and the city disappeared behind them.

"You've never heard of The Highlands?" Katie asked.

Jack shook his head. She explained that it was a gated community of mansions with its own church and police force in North Seattle.

Her friend Nancy was the live-in gardener for one of the mansion owners, who were out of town for the weekend, hence the party.

"So I should probably police my bottle caps, huh?" Jack asked jokingly. She laughed and agreed that would probably be a good idea.

They pulled off the highway, crossed Aurora, and drove into the dark quiet of the neighborhood around The Highlands. At the main gate they received a guest pass from the gatekeeper.

They drove down winding roads through tall evergreens. Mansions loomed out of the darkness on either side, each one more mansion-like than the one before. He wondered what was going on inside all of them. Some were dark. Lights were on in others. He tried to picture the decades of history contained in each mansion they passed.

Mansion life is how life is supposed to be, he thought. He wondered if he would ever earn his own mansion, but quickly put this line of thinking out of his head to enjoy the moment at hand when he realized he wasn't doing a single thing with his life that might result in owning a mansion.

"Here we are," she said as they pulled into the driveway of a cream-colored mansion surrounded on all sides by evergreens. She parked the car and after they got their backpacks, beer, and wine out of the trunk, they stood for a minute to take in the peaceful scene. Stars winked from behind the passing clouds. A soft but steady winter wind rustled through the branches of the fir trees. Jack breathed in a deep breath of fresh forest air.

There were a few other cars parked in front of the mansion. He didn't know how many people were going to show up, though she had told him there would probably be ten or twelve friends in all. The front door was unlocked and they walked inside.

There was a grand piano in the entryway and oil paintings on the walls. The mansion looked more like a museum inside than a house where people lived. Two dogs, a small one and a big one, ran to greet them at the door.

Jack and Katie walked into the kitchen where everyone was gathered. Nancy, Danielle and Taylor were sitting around the kitchen table. Everyone said hello and Nancy got up to stir the polenta she was cooking on the stove. A pleasant aroma of garlic and oregano filled the air. Nancy said that several of their friends had called to say they weren't going to make it and that no one else was coming. The night's five characters had been cast—five in a mansion on a Seattle U.S.A. Earth Friday night in the universe.

Jack opened bottles of Kilt Lifter Ale and handed one to Katie. Taylor took a small metal canister filled with green kind buds from her bag and proceeded to roll a joint, and even though Jack told himself he was going to abstain and stick to a beer or two, when the joint came his way he put it to his lips and took a big drag, and inhaled the smoke deep into his lungs. They were all quickly baked and Nancy began to make one funny comment after another as she worked at the stove and had all of them laughing.

She had roasted vegetables in olive oil and garlic and now spooned alternating layers of polenta and vegetables into a baking dish. Jack crumbled feta cheese on top of the last layer with a fork and Nancy returned the baking dish to the oven to heat the top to a crisp. Katie cut the bread and arranged it in a big wooden salad bowl with a dish of olive oil and chopped garlic in the middle. Danielle and Taylor prepared a salad in another big wooden bowl. When everything was ready, they brought it out to the dining room table, dimmed the chandelier, and lit the candles perched in silver holders.

Jack looked at the portrait of one of the house's matrons on the wall and raised his beer bottle to toast her presence. Taylor sparked a second joint after they took their places around the table, which they passed and smoked before eating. Jack exhaled a deep, stoned, relaxed breath and took in the beautiful scene. He suggested they should toast the moment.

Glasses clinked and sips of beer and wine were taken, after which they all fell into an eating trance interrupted every now and then by jokes and laughter. Jack felt time beginning to disappear as the combination of the night's company and ingredients worked their magic, and suddenly dinner was finished. They cleared the dishes and moved to a patio overlooking the back yard, where everyone but Jack smoked a cigarette.

After she finished her cigarette, Taylor rolled yet another joint and they smoked it there on the edge of the yard beneath the stars and trees. Jack stood behind them and stretched his legs and his back. He felt *really* relaxed and swayed to the rhythm of their voices and the wind rustling through the trees.

He leaned his head back and looked up at the stars. Just as he did so, a streaking yellow comet shot across the sky. The comet went on and on. When he held his hands up to measure its trail, it was more than three feet long, a lot of sky for a comet to streak across.

"Whooooahhhhhhh!" he said loudly. No one had seen it but him. How could they have missed it, it was right there! They looked at him with amused looks on their faces as he stammered while trying to describe it, too high to string together words. He wanted them to feel as excited about the comet as he was, but when he saw that they weren't, he tried to contain himself. The stars winked knowingly. The meteor was *his*.

After the last of the joint had been smoked, Nancy said it was time for the hot tub. Everything was happening so fast. Jack had barely started to digest his food. They walked downstairs, through the recreation room and outside to the hot tub patio. Nancy pulled the cover back and turned on the warm jets. The water glowed blue. His mind throbbed with the accumulation of euphoria.

The water bubbled around him. The jets massaged his back. The stars pulsed and twinkled above and the trees swayed in the wind. Toes touched beneath the surface of the water. He felt like he was in that painting with the nymphs in the pond.

After just ten minutes, they all yawned simultaneously. Food, the heat of the water, and a shared sense of complete relaxation had overwhelmed them. They got out of the hot tub and went back into the house, where they dried off and changed into their nightclothes. They returned to the TV room and Nancy put *Star Wars* into the VCR.

Twenty minutes into the film they all started to fall asleep. It was time for bed. Nancy told them to choose a bedroom. Jack walked into a room and turned on the lights. It was a kids' room with two twin beds and pictures of baseball players on the walls. He turned the light off and continued down the hall, where he found a couch in a room next to the kitchen and lay down.

The house cat came and settled on his chest. Whenever he shifted and moved, the cat maintained its balance and stayed perched on top of him, purring. Jack fell into a restless sleep until the sound of Nancy making coffee in the kitchen woke him up. He got up, read the paper, and talked to her about her life in the mansion. The others woke up one by one. Taylor and Danielle cooked a huge pan of curried potatoes. Eggs were cooked in another pan, toast in the toaster. They ate and talked and laughed about not making it through *Star Wars*.

When they were finished, Jack walked around the yard and took in the view of Puget Sound through the trees. The city and reality were far away. Time had moved so fast. It was time to go. Jack sighed. Katie started the car and pulled away from the mansion.

As they pulled through the gates and returned to the outside world, he said, "I don't want to go back to reality." Katie nodded in agreement.

They stopped at a dollar store and whittled away the morning in a slow motion haze of happy fatigue. The engine purred as they cruised down Aurora and Seattle appeared in view. Katie dropped him off at his apartment. Jack turned the key, opened the door, and walked inside. He looked around the place and thought, "no mansion here."

TENNIGUINESS

Jack was taking a late afternoon nap when he heard the phone ring as if from a great distance. He stood up and stumbled bleary-eyed to the phone. It was his friend Melissa. Jack had left a message on her answering machine the day before asking if she wanted to play tennis. She was calling him back to ask him if he wanted to play. He was tired today, though, and didn't feel like playing. They chatted for a few more minutes and said goodbye.

Jack yawned, stretched, and pulled himself out of his stupor. He remembered his promise to himself a few weeks earlier to say yes to offers the universe threw his way. He had been living an underground existence for too long while recovering from his break-up. It was time to start living again. He picked up the phone and called her back. Melissa said they would be playing "Tenniguinness" and that he should stop at the store to pick up a four-pack of Guinness beer on his way over. She would explain the rules later.

Jack gathered his racket and cans of balls from the closet, went to the supermarket for the beer, and headed over to Melissa's house, known as The Pagoda. The Pagoda seemed to possess some kind of charmed magic. In the five years he had known her, Jack ended up at The Pagoda a few times a year for the great parties that happened there. Once inside, it was like being in a faraway place with its own rules of time and space.

Miso, Melissa's friend's dog she was taking care of for the summer, was sitting on the grass in front of the house. Jack was always happy to see Miso and it seemed to Jack that Miso was always happy to see him.

"Miso!" Jack said, happy to see his friend. Miso ran over to say hello. Jack walked into the house and looked around. Everything was dark but for the light upstairs in Melissa's room.

"Hello?" Jack called into the darkness.

He walked up the stairs and found Melissa sitting at her desk. She was working with her "bug kit," an assortment of rubber stamps that depicted different bug parts.

She stamped them in ink and created bugs on paper. She picked up the sheet of paper she was working on and showed him the bugs she had made.

"Cool," Jack said.

Melissa seemed distant and unhappy. She spoke in circles, as if questioning herself and what she was saying while simultaneously making conversation.

"Maybe she's just stoned," Jack thought, looking at her pipe on the desk near the "bug kit."

They walked through the dusk and the neighborhood. There was a warm breeze blowing through the air. It was strange weather. Jack said that it reminded him of the New Orleans scene in Pirates Of The Caribbean at Disneyland where the fireflies fly around beneath a moonlit sky.

"Totally," Melissa said.

Miso ran ahead of them, stopping every now and then to sniff at something. When they arrived at the tennis courts, the lights were off and the button that was supposed to turn them on did not respond when they pressed it. They decided to play anyway in the light of the single streetlight next to the courts.

It was hard to see the ball, but they played as best they could, each with a can of Guinness in one hand, racket in the other. Miso ran around the court gathering up the balls and dropped them at their feet. After fifteen minutes of trying to use instinct to return the ball over the net, Jack suggested they take a break.

Jack opened up the airplane bottle of Bushmill's Irish Whiskey he had brought with the beer. They traded sips until it was gone, then opened their second cans of Guinness. Melissa produced a thick joint that was as big as Jack's middle finger and asked if he wanted to play "Cuban" style, a joint and can of beer in one hand, racket in the other.

They returned to the court. Jack lit the joint and took a few hits. He approached the net and handed the joint to Melissa, who stood there for a minute slowly inhaling its smoke before passing it back to Jack.

They hit a few balls back and forth, but as the effects of the pot settled in and the dimensions of the court began to mimic an abstract painting come to life, the quality of the tennis became secondary to the experience of the evening as a whole.

Jack watched as if from outside himself as the trees blended together with the stars, Miso and Melissa spoke their private language as they ran around the court, the breeze flowed like water over them, and the smoke transformed him from who he had been to who he really was.

He hit the balls that came his way back over the net, but he no longer felt connected to this simple act alone. It, in its turn, was connected to the ground at his feet, and the buzz in his head that had previously been filled with thoughts and observations was now vibrating with the mysterious whisperings of the spirits in the air around them.

As if by some prearranged cue, they both agreed they had played enough tennis. Jack packed up their trash in a bag and zipped up his racket in its case.

They walked silently back through the immaculate neighborhood past mansions and houses seemingly empty and dark but still projecting their presence onto the street as if they were alive. Jack took in every house they passed and tried to imagine the existence that would take place inside its walls were he to live there.

They walked slowly with their beers in hand, not speaking but listening and looking at the night, every now and then bumping into each other until they arrived back at The Pagoda, where they lit a single candle and smoked the rest of the joint sitting on the huge living room carpet.

Jack lay down on his back and stared up at the high ceiling. He looked at the patterns of shadow and light thrown off by the candle that made everything look like it was breathing and alive. Melissa lay on her stomach balanced on top of a blue exercise ball and rolled back and forth on the carpet with her arms outstretched as if flying.

After a toke from a second joint that had appeared in her hand, she rolled toward Jack and passed it to him. Jack stood up and sat down in the comfortable old armchair in the corner. It felt like a throne, The Pagoda a palace. High on one wall the wings that Melissa wore the previous Halloween hung from a nail and cast long shadows that made it appear to move and bob as if floating in midair.

There was a swing hung from a ceiling beam in one corner of the room. Melissa sat on it and began to rock gently back and forth. The rope creaked against the wood in rhythm with her movements. It was a beautiful scene—Melissa on the swing lit by the glow of the candle and the street lights outside, the wings hanging on the wall casting shadows above, Miso laying peacefully on the carpet, everything in the room seeming to breathe along with the calm summer night. Jack tried to imprint the moment into his memory to revisit later.

After they said good night, Jack walked home with his racket under his arm. His body pulsed with the ebb and flow of waves of marijuana energy, each one a new layer lifted to reveal an even deeper level of beauty behind it.

He stopped to look at the Space Needle from an intersection that provided a clear view. Its light pulsed through its structure like blood through veins. It was surrounded by stars and pointed to the sky and the infinite space beyond.

When Jack got home, he lit a candle, lay down on his couch and closed his eyes. The evening had cast a spell over him. His watched as his mind manufactured visions of places and things that melted into one another and became other things and other places. Each of these strange patterns and images seemed to have their own meaning that came from either the deep future or the deep past.

In the morning, they would be gone, but he would walk around all day bathed in the residue of what they had revealed—archaic metaphors, imagistic language, bundles of energy and light, the true language beyond the grasp of words at the edge of understanding, lessons as old and young as the past and future combined.

Jack fell into a deep sleep. The Earth moved through space and the universe exhaled a deep, calm breath and stretched beyond its own infinite expanse.

CODES

Jack walked out into the August night with few expectations except to see Crack Sabbath play at the 700 Club. Tuesday was the hardest night in Seattle to find the vibe of a good time, but if there was a show to see you could forgive the weekday its inherent lethargy and feel like you and the city were a little bit alive.

A cool breeze was blowing. Jack liked the way it felt on his skin. If nothing else, the night would provide this simple but pleasant sensation. He didn't know if he really felt like being out.

"Just stick to the plan," he told himself, and kept walking down Denny and onto Broadway, past the Bonney Watson funeral home, down Pine past Linda's, where it appeared to be a quiet lethargic evening, past the red glow of the Cha Cha, where he stopped and looked in the window but didn't see anyone he knew, and past the coffee drinkers sitting and talking at Bauhaus.

He stopped in front of the Baltic Room and pondered stopping there, but when he looked in the window and heard a tired jazz piano being played and tired drinkers with their heads leaned back against the wall as if they were falling asleep, he decided to keep moving towards his destination. He crossed the highway and looked at the lights of the skyscrapers rising into the starry night and the Space Needle's reassuring glow as it stood watch over the city.

As he approached the 700 Club, he could hear Skerik's saxophone floating out into the night. He crossed the street and entered the red glow of the stairway leading up to the club. A well-dressed doorman in a sharp suit checked his I.D. and asked for the $3 cover charge. As Jack handed him the bills, the doorman asked Jack how he was doing.

"I'm doing good," Jack said, leaving out all thoughts of lethargy and indecision. Once inside, he took a stool at a corner of the bar. The band played jazz standards and slow love ballads before they took their first break. Jack looked around the room. Everyone else was with someone, either as couples or with small groups of friends. It appeared he was the only one alone. The room was filled with talk. Jack wondered what they were all talking about.

The DJ played music with big beats and lots of bass during the break that got a few couples up and dancing. Elsewhere around the room, heads bobbed to the beat. People were starting to groove. There might have been lethargy elsewhere, but it felt like he'd found the night within the night.

When Crack Sabbath returned to the stage, they tore into some pretty intense stuff and people started to get down on the dance floor. Jack bobbed his head to the beat.

A woman on a date sitting on the stool on the other side of the corner of the bar was attempting to seduce her companion, who didn't seem to be picking up on her cues that she liked him.

When the guy stepped away from the bar to go to the restroom, she tried to light a match with one finger but the sulfur stuck to her skin and her thumb flared up briefly. Jack smelled burning flesh. She yelled out in pain and laughed at the same time as the music's chaos increased and enveloped the room with its madness.

"That's what you get for trying to be cool," Jack said, offering a piece of ice from his glass of water.

"I'm NOT cool," she insisted with a sigh, nursing her thumb in the bottom of her martini glass.

She ordered two more martinis. When her date returned, he now seemed to be warming up to her and looked her body up and down as she stood at the bar waiting for their drinks. They downed their martinis like they were water and ordered two more.

His eyes were glassy and stoned. Hers were clear, as if the alcohol hadn't affected her at all. When she put her ear to his mouth to hear what he was saying, she looked at Jack and smirked and rolled her eyes as if to say, "silly me."

When her date left the bar for another restroom stop, she stepped over to Jack and said, "He's all eyes and toes, that's all he can see."

"Are you guys on a first date?" Jack asked.

"He's doing a really good job," she said, almost apologetically.

Her date returned from the bar with two more martinis in hand. She threw her arms around his neck and kissed him passionately. Their tongues flashed in and out of each other's mouths as their hands moved over each other's bodies, seemingly choreographed by the crazy music.

Skerik was out of his mind and the drummer had moved into another realm. His hands and arms were a blur. The bassist was getting primal with his grooves and the dude at the Hammond organ reminded everyone that it was all a good time as he smiled and nodded with a look of sage wisdom in his eyes.

Jack went to the end of the bar to order a beer. A woman dressed in black sidled up to the bar and leaned against him as if she knew him.

What was her code? He'd seen her on the other side of the bar in a group of people who were friends of friends of his, at one point sitting on the lap of one of the guys in the group while running her hands through his hair. Jack asked her if she was having a good Tuesday night.

"I'm having a good time," she said.

"Tuesday's usually a pretty hard night to have a good time," Jack said.

She leaned her face in towards his and said, as if it was a secret, "it's a tough nut to crack."

Jack laughed, paid for his drink, and returned to his barstool, unsure of what their interaction had been about. He turned his attention away from the band and looked back at the bar, where she now stood talking to another guy who was about to order a drink. They were laughing about something and when the bartender poured and slid two shots across the bar, they clinked glasses and tossed them back. The guy returned to his table of friends and she returned to her table in the corner, where she once again sat on the lap of the guy she was with.

Jack walked out of the bar and into the night after the band had played its last bit of chaos and the doorman had given everyone the bad news that it was time to go home.

On the corner, an Irish woman was making out with an Irish guy. Jack knew they were Irish because when they stopped kissing, the woman held the guy's face, made him look her in the eyes, and insisted, in a thick Irish accent, "it's just you and me, you and me!"

"I know, love," the guy said in his own thick Irish accent, "I know." They returned to making out as Jack walked up the street towards home.

LONGING (DESIRE)

There were nights when the whole city was alive. More nights, though, were strange landscapes of restless lethargy and what felt like double gravity.

Jack decided to take the bus to Queen Anne, but the vibe there was the same as on Capitol Hill. At the Mecca, three guys at the table next to his yawned and talked about how tired they were.

"Good luck," the bartender said when he pushed Jack's pint glass towards him across the bar.

Jack sipped his beer, listened to the jukebox music, and looked for signs that the night was going to make an effort to congeal into something tangible.

He had the feeling that he was sitting amongst ghosts in a haunted bar and decided to leave and go to the 700 Club to listen to some live music instead.

If there was nothing doing there, then he'd know there was nothing doing anywhere and that he should just call it a night and probably should have called it a night from the start.

He left his unfinished pint behind, walked across the street, looked in the window of Sorry Charlie's where a few regulars he recognized from previous visits on more lively nights were singing at the piano bar, and leaned against the wall to wait for the downtown bus. The Space Needle hovered nearby.

A woman wearing burgundy jeans, thigh high suede boots, and an amber leather jacket crossed the street towards him. Her short hair was dyed platinum blonde and she had striking steel blue eyes. She looked at the bus stop schedule, asked Jack what time it was, and leaned against the wall next to him. They were waiting for the same bus.

She told Jack she worked at a nearby restaurant and had stayed after her shift was over to drink wine with the owner. Now she didn't know whether to go home or try to find some of her friends at a club downtown.

"It's a strange night," Jack said.

"There's a feeling of longing in the air," she said.

That was it exactly, Jack thought. When the bus came, they sat next to each other and continued talking. She said she was a dancer and performed at a club in Pioneer Square. She suggested he come the following Saturday to see her and said that he could meet a whole new crowd and be part of a whole new scene. He thought to himself that this was exactly what he needed.

When they got off the bus downtown, she said she was getting a "psychic vibe" telling her she had to get going. She hailed a cab, told him find her and say hello the following week, and disappeared into the night.

Jack walked up 1st Ave towards the Showbox. Two drunk women swayed from side to side on the sidewalk ahead. As they walked past, one swayed towards him and asked, "We're not swaying, are we?"

"No," Jack said, "it's the ground that's swaying."

Made in the USA
San Bernardino, CA
01 October 2018